SALAAM MEANS PEACE

Malak Abaroui
Salaam Means Peace

Published by Spines
ISBN: 979-8-89691-501-0

SALAAM MEANS PEACE

MALAK ABAROUI

To Prophet Muhammad ﷺ, the man whose legacy continues to enlighten the hearts of his ummah.

And to my HIC family: Not a day goes by that I don't pray to Allah for Him to unite us in Jannah inshaAllah. No matter where life takes us, I will always love you all more than I can ever express.

CONTENTS

PROLOGUE

Many have asked me to share my story—the story of how I became an activist and an internet sensation. As much as I want to share every single detail of what has happened to me, I can't, because the truth is, this story is not mine alone.

It is the story of the family I loved and lost. The story of the family that took me in when I had nothing. And it is the story of many who have been deprived of their basic right to religious freedom.

Looking back at everything I've been through, I think if someone had told my fourteen-year-old self that, in just one year, my life would change the way it did, I would have laughed in their face. But my life did change. I changed. And through that change, with some help, I was able to change the lives of many.

As painful as some parts of it were, I wouldn't alter any part of my journey. It was, indeed, a thrilling one.

I am Muhammad Arshad, and this is my story.

CHAPTER 1

I stared at the bright sun, letting its rays sting my eyes. It burned. Instinctively, I closed them—then forced them open again, welcoming the pain, willing the tears to come.

I didn't care if I lost my eyesight. At that moment, nothing mattered.

I felt a pang of hatred for everything around me. The world that I had once loved had taken everything from me, and I despised it for that. The trees, the children walking by, the grass, the street—every single thing in existence irritated me in ways I couldn't explain.

I felt dead without actually dying. Like my soul was trapped in a different dimension, and my body was nothing more than an empty husk. Simple nothingness, functioning on autopilot.

For months, I had been drowning in this state—bitter,

angry at the world for what it had stolen from me. I once had a life that, to others, may not have seemed like much. But to me, it was everything. A mother, a father, a sister, a stable home. Things I now know to be a luxury.

I had a loving family. My parents were amazing. My sister, Maryam, was amazing. While most of my friends described their younger sisters as annoying or immature, I never saw Maryam that way. She was my best friend, my confidant—the one person I could always count on.

My parents were both lawyers, and despite their busy schedules, they always made time for us. Maryam and I went to the same school, and both of us had great friend groups. We would often hang out at each other's houses or meet up in different places around the city.

I was the captain of my basketball team. A straight-A student. The golden child of our community.

We were all Muslims, and Islam was woven into every part of our lives. My mom and Maryam both wore the hijab. Everything we did was halal. And we were happy. We had no one but each other, and that was enough. We were taught that if we followed Islamic principles, we would find ultimate happiness.

But we didn't.

Because in a single night, everything I loved was taken from me.

No warning. No time to prepare. Just… gone.

Leaving me lost, confused, struggling to process what had happened—what to do next. Clutching onto a thin rope of faith, one that was fraying with every passing second.

It had started as a normal day. Looking back, I regret not cherishing that normalcy. I regret not savoring every single minute. Now, all I had were memories, and I found myself clinging to them with everything I had.

I had woken up excited because it was Friday, and I was going to my best friend Ahmad's house after school. I got dressed—black Nike t-shirt, basketball shorts—grabbed my black Nike Elite backpack (a birthday gift from Ahmad), and headed downstairs for breakfast.

Dad was just leaving. I hugged him—a quick, casual hug. Not the tight, lingering hug I wish I had given him.

"Bye, Dad," I said.

I wish I had told him I loved him. I wish I had held on longer. I wish I had asked if he was proud of me—proud of my grades, my basketball skills, my Quran studies.

But it never crossed my mind that this would be the last time I'd see him.

Yes, we all know life is unpredictable. We know there's always a chance we won't return when we step out the door. That every goodbye could be the last.

But do we *really* know it? Do we *really* think about it?

If we did, wouldn't we make every moment, every word, every touch matter so much more?

He kissed the top of my head. "Bye, Mo. I love you."

I love you. Those were his last words to me.

I knew he loved me. But did he know I loved him? Did I say it enough? Show it enough?

I would spend the rest of my life wondering.

I locked the door behind him and went to the kitchen. Mom was home—one of those rare mornings when she didn't have to work. She was making breakfast.

"Assalamualaikum," I said, hugging her before sitting down.

Maryam was already at the table, eating. I gave her a light punch on the shoulder. She punched me back. That was our greeting.

"Salaam, sleepyhead. Aren't you gonna eat anything?" she asked.

"Good morning to you too, dear sister," I replied sarcastically. "Why yes, I *am* going to consume something in order to fuel my body. Thank you for your deep concern over my dietary needs."

She laughed and punched me again.

"Mom, are you picking me up from Ahmad's place later?"

"Can you take the bus back? I have to drop Maryam off at the masjid for Quran class, and I want to stay and listen in. Dad will probably meet us there, and we'll drive home together. You might be alone for a few hours."

If only I had known then how drastically my life would change in those few hours.

"That's alright," I said, grabbing a granola bar and

unwrapping it. "I'll see you tonight then. Assalamualaikum."

Then she came over and hugged me.

For the last time.

She tried to kiss my cheek, but I pulled away, so she just ruffled my hair.

"Walaikum Assalam."

Walaikum Assalam. It was a standard reply to a standard Muslim greeting. But now, I really think about what it means—really absorb the weight of the words.

Peace be upon you.

The very last thing my mother had said to me was a wish for peace. Salaam. Peace. I value peace so much now because of that. I try to spread it as much as possible. But how can I, when I haven't found peace for myself?

And I know I never will—not until I am reunited with her. With all of them.

Looking back at that moment, I wish I had let her kiss me. I wish I had hugged her tightly and told her I loved her. I wish I had asked her one last question.

But I didn't know.

How could I have known?

And even if I did—what could I have asked? What could she have answered?

Sometimes I wish I knew. Other times, I realize that knowing would have made it unbearable. The days leading up to it would have been torture. I would have gone insane if I had known that was the last time I would ever see my mom. The last time I would be able to bury my face in her arms and inhale the familiar scent of perfume mixed with Dove soap and Moroccan argan oil.

The woman I loved the most.

I was a part of her. That kind of bond is supposed to be unbreakable.

Yet death managed to break it.

I waited for Maryam to say goodbye, put on her shoes, and adjust her hijab. She had just started wearing it recently. She spent months researching the importance of hijab before declaring herself ready. I remember the first day she wore it. She was terrified, tugging her hood over her head, refusing to leave my side.

I had wrapped her in a hug and told her she had this.

I wish I had told her I was proud of her. That she looked beautiful in it. That I admired her courage to wear her faith for the world to see.

But I never got the chance.

Or maybe I had the chance and never took it.

Once she was ready, we left and started walking to school. Ridgmore High—grades six through twelve. I was in ninth grade. Maryam was in eighth.

It was June. Just a few weeks until summer break.

We walked slowly, the heat blazing down on us. I don't remember what we talked about. I just remember that Maryam couldn't stop talking, and I kept nodding, pretending to listen.

The truth?

I was thinking about what I would do with Ahmad that afternoon.

I wish I had paid more attention. Soaked up everything she had to say. She always had a lot to say, and all of it was valuable. So, so valuable.

Her advice, her ideas—they got me through some of my darkest times. She was always there for me.

And I failed to be there for her.

I failed as an older brother.

When we got to school, I said goodbye and started walking toward my friends.

But she stopped me.

She wrapped her arms around me.

"I love you," she said. "You know that, right?"

"I know," I replied. "And I love you too."

I love you too.

At least I got to tell Maryam that I loved her. I'll never know if I showed it the way I should have. But I hope she knew I meant it.

She was my sister. My second half. My best friend.

We went through life together, and she always had my back.

The day she died, a part of me died too. A part I will never get back.

I watched until she reached her friends, making sure she was safe. Then, I turned to mine.

My friends were all great, but I was especially close to Ahmad. We met when we started doing hifz together at the masjid. Then, we ended up in the same middle school. Our families were close, and we always hit it off.

For about ten minutes, we talked about what now seems like nonsense—who got what grade, which teacher was the worst, whose house we'd watch the Lakers game in, what we'd do over the weekend.

Before we knew it, it was time for class.

I said goodbye to everyone, then headed inside. It was a normal school day. I had a few tests, got assigned a history project, and was given a lot of homework—which I remember complaining about to Ahmad during lunch. I wish I hadn't complained but had instead appreciated the fact that homework was my biggest problem at the time. But how could I have known that the next day, it would be the least of my worries?

After lunch, I headed to my afternoon classes—my favorites. I had chemistry and biology, subjects I enjoyed because I wanted to major in biochemistry in college. The hours dragged on, but finally, the school day ended. I raced outside to the courtyard to wait for Ahmad. His older brother, Imran, was picking us up. While we waited, we played a little basketball.

When Imran arrived, we piled into the car, and he drove us home. At Ahmad's house, we raced upstairs to his room, played Roblox for a while, then went outside for more basketball. Later, his mom called us in for dinner, and we ate like there was no tomorrow.

When it was time to leave, I was about to catch the

bus when Imran offered to drop me off. I agreed, and Ahmad decided to tag along. Once we arrived, I thanked them, said salaam, and went inside.

I sat down in the kitchen and started my homework. After about an hour of powering through geometry, I heard a knock on the door.

The knock that changed everything.

To this day, I am averse to knocks.

Confused—since I knew my family wouldn't be back yet—I got up and cautiously opened it. A police officer stood before me. The moment I saw him, my heart dropped.

"Are you Muhammad Arshad?"

I nodded, unable to speak.

When he told me the news, I stood frozen for a few seconds before collapsing to my knees, screaming at the top of my lungs. My mouth felt like sand, my eyes dry. I longed for tears—to release something, anything—but I was numb. The officer knelt beside me, placing a hand on my shoulder. The pain didn't build gradually; it crashed over me like an unstoppable wave, drowning me in an instant.

He pleaded with me to breathe slowly, but I couldn't think.

"Muhammad, calm down."

His voice was deep but somber, gentle yet firm. I remember nothing else about him—not his name, face, or even his height. Only the weight of his hand grounding me and the sound of his voice tethering me to reality.

"Remember Me, and I will remember you. Praise Me and do not disbelieve."

The Quranic verse echoed in my mind, holding me together as I struggled to grasp what had happened.

We drove to the hospital as fast as we could.

It was too late.

Mom and Dad had died in a car accident on their way home from the masjid.

I raced to the children's unit to check on Maryam, but a doctor stopped me.

She was gone too.

I saw her lifeless body being wheeled away. Pushing past the doctor, I ran for a final glimpse of my sister. Her once rosy cheeks were now pale. Strands of her light brown hair escaped from her hijab, and I gently tucked them back into place. I bent down and kissed her forehead, my tears mixing with the dried blood on her face. Pressing my palm against her cheek, I held her cold fingers, burying my face into her chest.

"Ya Allah, how could You do this to me?"

"I love you," I whispered. "I love you, I love you, I love you."

Hoping, somehow, she could still hear me.

I made the doctor promise not to remove her hijab in front of men. My little sister may have been gone, but I wouldn't let her be stripped of her dignity. Islam was the center of her life, as it was mine. Everything about her radiated faith.

I watched as they wheeled her away, slowly, inevitably. She was being pulled from me, yet she still tugged at my heart, ripping it from my chest and placing it into hers—because Maryam was a part of me, and I was a part of her. We completed each other.

And now, I would never see her again.

I would live with only half a heart.

"Goodbye, Muhammad," I could almost hear her say.

"Please, no. Don't say goodbye. Not now. Not ever."

Without thinking, I ran.

Past the doctor who tried to stop me.

"Muhammad, stop!"

His voice grew more distant, like a fading echo.

I ran past the nurses pleading for me to stay calm, past the police officers chasing after me. It didn't matter. I had to get away. I had to find my family.

That lifeless body wasn't my sister.

I didn't know where I was running—I was just running. As if, by some miracle, my sorrow would fall away along the path. As if, if I ran fast enough, I could find them again.

"They're gone."

I kept telling myself.

"They never belonged to you to begin with. They're with Allah, stupid."

"To God we belong, and to Him we return."

It was the phrase every Muslim recites upon hearing of a death. Words I had spoken many times before.

Yet still, I kept thinking—

If I go home, maybe Maryam will be there in the dining room, doing homework.

Maybe Mom will be in the kitchen, cooking dinner.

Maybe—just maybe—this was all a mistake.

Maybe they weren't really gone.

I would walk in, and she would smile one of her warm smiles and hug me. Then I would sit down next to Maryam to finish my homework. Only this time, I would hug her tighter, stroke her hair. Help her with her work. Then we would talk about anything and everything.

We would sit down together for dinner, and once we were done, we would clean the kitchen. I would splash her face with soapy dishwater, and she would chase me with a mop.

But those days were gone.

I could only relive them in my head, catching glimpses of the joy held by the memories. My family was gone, and I would never get them back. This was a reality that would take me years to face.

The next few days were a blur. I don't remember much of what happened. I was completely numb during the funeral—when I had to say goodbye to my old life, when I said goodbye to Ahmad and his family, when I visited Maryam's and my parents' graves. I didn't dare go near the masjid.

I was numb when I was put into the foster care system.

I was numb when I was told I would have to move all the way to New York due to the lack of housing in my area.

I was numb when all of my family's possessions were sold, the money used to pay for the funeral expenses. The rest was put into a bank account for me to access when I turned eighteen.

What would I do with that money? They might as well lock it up forever. It held no value.

I didn't know how to react or process any of it. So I didn't react at all.

How are you supposed to deal with being told to pack up your life in a single suitcase? How do you deal with never seeing your family again? How are you supposed to survive on your own at fifteen?

I didn't know the answer to any of these.

I didn't want to know.

I never thought I would have to know.

All I knew was that my life had been completely turned upside down. My sense of stability crushed into smithereens.

"Hey, Muhammad, where were you?"

Brian, my new younger foster brother. The first time I saw him, he immediately reminded me of Maryam. The same light brown hair. The same dark eyes filled with ambition and love for the world.

Like Maryam, he tried his best to make me feel at ease, to get me to open up. Maryam could always sense when something was wrong. She had a way of getting me to talk.

I could tell Brian was the same way.

Even though I loved him, even though I wanted to be his older brother, I couldn't let him know that. I could never let anyone get close to me again.

I had already failed at being an older brother once. I couldn't do it again.

I cut myself off from everyone. My friends back home eventually stopped trying to reach me. Even Ahmad. That hurt the most.

I did it out of fear—fear of losing someone else, fear of having to go through that pain all over again.

"None of your business," I mumbled, running into my room and slamming the door behind me.

I grabbed Maryam's journal from my bag.

She had filled it with stories, diary entries, little pieces of herself. I found it in her room the day before I moved, and I had carried it with me ever since. Every time a wave of sadness overtook me, I would open it and read a little.

That day, I read an entry she had written not long before she died:

"Sometimes we work so hard and do so much that we forget that nothing is permanent. This world is temporary. Our existence is temporary. The only thing that is permanent is God."

It was like she knew. Like she sensed that something was going to happen.

Yet she had seemed so happy. So normal.

Something was bothering her, and she didn't tell me.

I thought we told each other everything. I was supposed to be there for her.

I couldn't read anymore.

I flung the book across the room and sat there, numb.

It wasn't fair.

None of it was fair.

I closed my eyes and began to remember my mother —how kind and gentle she was. She was full of love for everyone. Everything she did was filled with unconditional love. She was a nurturer, the glue that held our family together with her quiet strength.

I thought of my dad. He was a protector, his fierce strength keeping our family safe. He was always ready for a good game of basketball, a morning run around the neighborhood, or sometimes just a talk. Those talks would always put me at ease. I emulated him greatly, wanting to be like him in every way—yet his strength failed that day.

I thought of Maryam. She was funny and empathetic, wise beyond her years. She was always ready to give me advice when I needed it. Sometimes, it felt like she was the older sibling.

How could this happen? How could they leave me

when I needed them most? How could they go when I loved them so much?

Suddenly, a knock on the door interrupted my thoughts.

"Muhammad, can I come in?"

It was Brian.

"Ugh, fine. What is it?"

"You looked upset coming in. What's up?"

"None of your concern."

"But—"

"Shut up and get out of my room!"

"I just wanted to talk, bro."

He looked at me—perplexed, concerned—like he wanted to say more but didn't know how. Instead, he closed the door and left.

I could hear Mike talking to him through the thin apartment walls.

"Brian, let him be. He's going through a lot right now. It's not easy on him."

The care my new family offered was a mediocre reimbursement for all that I had lost.

The next day was Monday, and I was back at school. I had always been a straight-A student, and even with everything going on, I still maintained my grades and paid attention in class. School, in many ways, was an escape.

I had developed a routine in my new life. Wake up. Get dressed. Head out. I tried to deal with the hurt, the loss, the grief by not giving it any thought. I blocked it out, focused on consistency. The routine gave me a sense of stability.

"Alhamdulillah, Allah blessed us with two children because Muhammad paved the way for us to have another."

My parents frequently told their friends this. Even as a kid, I had maintained stability, always keeping my eyes on the prize, always inspiring Maryam to do the same.

Brian tried to get me to walk with him to school, but I ignored him and took another way. Then I would come home, finish my homework, and wash up for dinner.

Dinner was difficult, living with a non-Muslim family. I only ate halal. But they knew that, and they always made sure there was something for me. I never asked them to. They just did it.

After dinner, I would go up to my room. Today was no different—except this time, Mike came up and tried to talk to me.

I had been isolating myself. Talking with Mike and Brian forced me to face my reality, something I wasn't ready to do. So I avoided contact, hoping they wouldn't notice me.

"Hey, Muhammad."

"Hi."

"So, how was school?"

I ignored him.

"Brian told me what happened between you two."

"And?"

"Muhammad, I can see that you're hurting. I can't even begin to imagine what you're going through, especially at your age. And I want to be here for you. We all do. But we can't if you don't let us."

"I don't need any help. I don't need anyone!"

But didn't I?

As a Muslim, I was fully reliant on Allah. I knew first-hand the meaning of true vulnerability. Yet even after all these months, I still hadn't learned how to properly stand without leaning on someone else.

CHAPTER 2

I was unable to sleep that night, so I got up and went to my bookshelf. It took me a while, but I finally found what I was looking for—my Quran. I traced my fingers over the black leather cover, feeling the familiar curves of the Arabic letters. I loved that Quran; it was the one Mom gave me when I first started doing *hifz*. It had been a gift from my father when they made *umrah* together for the first time, shortly after they were married. Maryam had the same one, but in pink.

I closed my eyes, remembering the day of my *hifz* graduation last year—the ceremony in which I was declared a *hafiz*, meaning I had memorized the entire book. I turned the pages to find Surah Yaseen, the surah I had recited that day. I remembered standing before my community, my parents by my side, as the imam bent down to place a medal of honor around my neck. He exited the stage, and I was handed a microphone.

"Bismillah al-Rahman al-Raheem." I began, my voice low and uncertain. It was intimidating, standing before so many people whose knowledge of Islam far surpassed mine. Despite all the effort I had dedicated to achieving such a monumental goal, my understanding felt limited. Then I glanced at Maryam. She was smiling, giving me a thumbs-up. I smiled back, realizing that was all the reassurance I needed.

In the name of Allah, the Compassionate, the Merciful.

I began to recite, my voice filling the hall. Surah Yaseen was often called the heart of the Quran; it contained all the essential lessons of the book. It was also my favorite. I wanted to go back to that day, even if only for a moment.

Slowly, I began to read. At first, I was hesitant, as if the words were too much for my tongue to release, too much for my soul to bear. But as I went on, my voice grew stronger. Eventually, I stopped reading, closed the book, and held it close to my chest. Then, I started reciting from memory—just as I had that day.

This was the book of all Muslims, the last book of guidance revealed to mankind. And now, I carried it in my heart. After years of hard work, I had finally absorbed its message. I swore to myself that I would become a walking version of the Quran, that I would act by its teachings so that people would read them through me.

When I finished, I was in a daze, in awe. It felt as though I had been transported back to that moment. Then, I got the sensation that someone was listening. I looked up.

It was Mike.

"What was that song?" he asked.

"That wasn't a song," I responded coldly.

So much for acting by the teachings of the Quran. It taught the use of gentle language and respect, but in that moment, I didn't have it in me to possess either. Not right now.

"Well, whatever it was, it was beautiful. You have an amazing voice."

With that, he exited the room, leaving me to spiral back into my thoughts.

Maryam was so close to finishing the Quran. She was on Surah Baqarah—the longest and hardest surah to memorize. The day she died, she had been coming home from *hifz* class at the *masjid*.

I remembered what my mom used to say. Until I was about seven or eight, she tucked me into bed every night and shared an Islamic teaching. I was supposed to fall asleep thinking about how I could relate to it or implement it in my life.

That night, she had said:

"Allah does not give us burdens greater than we can bear. If He gives us an obstacle that seems too big or scary to overcome, know that He believes we can handle it. Allah tests us. He gives

us trials to see if we truly deserve the reward of Paradise. When life feels overwhelming, take comfort in the fact that Allah has honored you with such a trial. When Allah chooses to test you, accept the pain with great honor."

I remember lying in bed that night, wondering what that truly meant. What tests awaited me?

Who would have known that, seven years later, I would come face to face with the answer in the worst way imaginable?

Now, more than ever, I realize how valuable those lessons were. I realize how valuable life is. How valuable Islam is.

Without Islam, I wouldn't have made it. I would have found myself chasing my family, spiraling down a never-ending hole just to join them. But because of Islam, I only chase Allah.

I have learned to rely on Him alone because He has taught me that people—willingly or unwillingly—will leave. But He never will.

He took my family because they belong to Him, because He wanted them back.

He took them from me because He loves me, and He wants me to turn to Him.

Turning to Him, keeping His book close to my chest, and His words on the tip of my tongue—these are the only ways I can even remotely function on a day-to-day basis.

Yet sometimes, even that comfort isn't enough to ease my aching heart.

And at the same time, the bitter reality is too much to bear.

Reading his book wasn't enough. I got up, grabbed my prayer mat, and sat on it. I had already completed my nightly prayers, but it wasn't enough—at least not tonight. I needed to talk to Allah.

He is the one who created me and guided me.
He is the one who feeds me and gives me water.
And if I am sick, He is the one who cures me.
He is the one who will cause me to die and then revive me.

My Lord, grant me wisdom and make me among the righteous.

Ya Allah, I memorized Your book word for word. I implemented Your teachings one by one. I know You test those who believe. I know You want to test my imaan. Please don't let it falter.

You took them away from me so I could rely solely on You. And now, You are all I have, ya Rabbi.

CHAPTER 3

The next day was a school day, and my routine was no different from how it had always been. I got up, made minimal contact with my foster family, and left to start the day. I swiped my metro card, got onto the subway, and made my usual half-hour trip to school.

It's crazy how fast some things become routine. I hadn't been doing this for very long, yet it already felt familiar—natural, even. It gave me an odd sense of comfort, knowing that despite all this change, one thing could stay consistent. I was functioning on autopilot, and for once, it was nice to give my brain a break.

Yet, there was always this lingering thought: what if what I had become accustomed to suddenly changed? In an instant, I could lose everything I had gotten used to. I never thought my life would be uprooted so rapidly. But then again, I grew up being taught to put my trust fully in

Allah's plan. As disheartening as it was, I tried to do it once more—for the sake of my family and, more importantly, for the sake of Allah. That is the beauty of Islam. We live for the sake of Allah. We love Him, and everything we do is for Him and Him only.

Once I arrived at my stop, I made my way to Willow Heights High School. I went to one of the most elite schools in New York City. Keeping up with the curriculum had been somewhat difficult. A guidance counselor from my old school had told me I was on track to graduate as valedictorian. That probably wouldn't happen now. The curriculum here was brutal, and the competition was high.

I still tried, though. School was one of the only things I put all my energy into. When I was solving math equations, I didn't have to think about anything except getting to the answer. When I was reading, I wasn't thinking about my life or anything around me—I was only lost in what would happen next. When I was studying history, I was absorbed in what had come before me. But once I left school, I had to face the dreaded present.

When I got to my first-period class, everything was normal. Kids were talking, papers were scattered around, and textbooks sat on each of our desks. After every test in history class, we previewed the next unit by reading from the textbooks, so I thought nothing of it. I sat down and began taking notes, struggling to push yesterday out of my brain.

Then, all of a sudden, the principal, Mr. Garcia, walked in. He stood in front of the room and announced that our history teacher, Mr. Davis, was taking a temporary leave due to personal reasons. Until then, we would have a substitute.

"Class, I would like to introduce Mr. Carter," he said.

A tall, thin man with deadly pale skin and piercing blue eyes walked in. He looked intimidating—the kind of teacher who meant business. He wore a dark brown suit and a red tie. In his hand, he carried a black briefcase, which he set down on the large desk in front of the room.

"Good morning, everyone. I am Mr. Carter, and I will be your teacher," he said in a cold voice.

At this point, after everything I had been through, nothing really scared me or even mattered to me anymore. I just thought, *Cool, another teacher here to do his job.* But if he didn't show respect, that was going to be a problem.

"I will start off today by taking attendance. Muhammad Arshad?"

I raised my hand. He glared at me and gave me a look of disgust.

"Samuel Brooks?"

Sam, a small kid who could pass for 14 instead of 16, raised his hand. His bush of blond hair stuck up in all directions. Sam had tried to befriend me several times, but I was still wary of letting people get close, so I ignored him for the most part.

"Your teacher has asked me to give you back your exams from last week," Mr. Carter announced. "Most of you did very well. Some, however… not so much."

He said the last part with a smug smile, as if the news pleased him. One by one, he handed back our tests. I, of course, had gotten an A.

Sam was looking over my shoulder, trying to sneak a glance at my grade.

I flipped my paper over. "Turn around and mind your own damn business!" I snapped.

"Quiet!" Mr. Carter yelled. "I do not tolerate that kind of behavior in my classroom."

I scowled and turned away from him. I wanted to yell, to protest, to respond, but then I thought of Maryam and what she would have wanted me to do.

"Silence," she had once said, "is the best possible revenge. It lets your enemy know that you don't care."

I had always thought that was dumb—something an adult would say just to avoid confrontation. But today, I welcomed it. It seemed like it would work on someone like Mr. Carter. Besides, he was a teacher. There wasn't much else I could do.

I pretended to focus on reviewing my test, but in reality, my mind was racing.

I didn't know why I was acting this way or how to change it, but I hated it. It felt like I was trapped in a dark room, with a door right in front of me, yet I couldn't reach it because I was chained to the wall.

The wall of my sorrow. The wall of my grief.

The wall that had taken me hostage and refused to let me rejoin my family.

Before I could get to the door, I had to break the chain.

But I had no idea how.

During lunch, I sat at my usual table, isolated from everyone, when Brian approached me. He was a freshman in high school and had gotten into Willow Heights last year by scoring a 615 on the admissions test—a feat that was incredibly hard to achieve. The kid was smart, like really smart.

He sat down across from me and opened his bag, reaching inside to pull out a package wrapped in sky-blue paper.

"This is for you," he said. "My mom and I got it the other day, and I wanted to be the one to give it to you. Open it."

I hesitated before taking the package. Slowly, I peeled off the wrapping paper and found a brown leather notebook.

"What is this?" I asked.

"Muhammad, you're hurting. I don't blame you, but you're not talking to anyone, and bottling it all up isn't healthy. If you can't talk, then write. It'll do you good."

"I've already said it before, and I'll say it again—I don't need help from anyone!"

"Muhammad, please!" His voice wavered. "I'm missing

class for this. I want to help you because you need it. You say you don't, but you do. You can ignore me for the rest of your life after this—just please take the book!"

His eyes brimmed with tears. I had never seen him cry before, and it hurt to see him like that. A different kind of hurt. One I hadn't felt in a long time. I welcomed it, though, because it reminded me that there were still people I might care about—and who apparently cared about me.

My expression softened. I stood up to leave but took the book with me.

I headed to the library, found a table, and sat down. I opened the notebook, took out a pen, and began to write. Words poured out of me, one emotion dragging the next onto the page. I wrote so much, so fast, that frustration crept in—my hand couldn't keep up with my thoughts.

When I finally stopped, the numbness I had carried for so long was gone. In its place was raw, unfiltered grief. My feelings were so tender, so exposed, that I felt defenseless, like anything could hurt me and I wouldn't be able to stop it. My hands trembled. The pen slipped from my grasp and hit the floor.

I buried my head in my arms and began to cry—right there in the empty library.

Arms wrapped around me, holding me tight. A hand rested on my shoulder.

"It's okay," Brian said softly. "Bro, I'm here."

I looked up. Brian and Sam stood there, watching me, waiting for me to say something.

"Are you alright now?" Sam asked.

I nodded, pulled away from Brian, and gathered my things. I had math next. On my way, I stopped in the bathroom to wash my face.

When I stepped out, I felt better than I had in a long time.

After school, I got a text from Mike saying he would be late home from work today, so Brian and I had to figure out dinner. When I got home, I set some pasta to boil for spaghetti and went to my room to change. When I was done, I plugged my phone in to charge, grabbed the leather notebook Brian gave me, and went to the living room.

I continued writing. Some of it was serious—full of deep, intense emotions—while some of it was just nonsense and random thoughts. But it still felt good to get all of it out nonetheless. It reminded me of how Maryam would always be writing in her journal, encouraging me to do the same, though I never did. I wondered if she got the same comfort from it as I did. At that moment, I promised myself that no matter how long it took, I would share Maryam's story with the world. I would dedicate the rest of my life to making her legacy known.

I went back into the kitchen to find that the pasta had finished cooking. I strained it, set it aside, and began working on the sauce. I remembered how Mom never used anything from a box or jar—her cooking was always from scratch. She taught me everything I knew about cooking. I could still picture myself at five years old, watching her cook. She started me off with basic kitchen safety, then gradually introduced me to the actual cooking.

I dug some tomatoes out of the fridge and began chopping them. Then I grabbed some onions and cilantro.

"Do you need some help?"

I looked up. It was Brian.

We both worked in silence. I brushed past him, gathering all the spices from the cabinets along with some tomato paste, then assembled everything in the pan. I turned down the heat and watched the sauce simmer.

"Should I start putting this away?" Brian asked.

"Yeah," I replied, adding a bit more olive oil to the pan.

When the sauce was ready, I mixed in the pasta. I filled two plates and set them on the kitchen table. Brian and I sat down to eat, but the silence between us felt heavier than before.

I couldn't bring myself to eat. Everything reminded me of my family—especially food. No matter how busy we were, we always made time to sit down together for meals. And now, even that was gone. Nothing would ever bring us together again.

For the rest of my life, I would simply drag forward, waiting for the akhirah—the day I could embrace them once again.

I left my plate untouched and went to my room. There, I dug out Maryam's journal and started reading.

Today, I finished memorizing Surah Yaseen. It has been my favorite Surah ever since I heard Muhammad recite it at his hifz graduation a few weeks ago. I promised myself that no matter what, I would memorize it so that someday I could recite it at my graduation as well. It's still hard to believe that it's almost here. I only have a few more surahs left to memorize before completing hifz. Just a few years ago, I never would have imagined coming this far. Memorizing Quran was never something I considered until Muhammad started doing it, but now, I'm glad I did. So many good things came out of it. I became more connected to my religion and even started wearing hijab afterward—

A sudden knock at the door made me stop reading.

I assumed it was Mike—he should be home by now—but no, it was Brian.

"Can I come in?"

"Sure."

"You haven't eaten anything all day. Please, come back and eat."

"Why do you care?" I retorted, refusing to acknowledge his concern. I turned back to the journal. "You can go now."

"Why shouldn't I?"

I sighed. "Look, I'm getting really annoyed with you constantly following me around. You think you can replace my family, but you're wrong—you can't. You think I can just get over what happened? But no, I can't. And you can't help me. So please, bro, leave me alone."

He started walking into the room, but then I got up and punched him in the chest. Hard. So hard that I knocked him down against the door.

He looked at me, appalled. Stunned—like he hadn't fully processed what had just happened. I waited for him to get up, to hit me back, to say something. But he just sat there, frozen.

Eventually, he got up.

"Brian, I—"

He ignored me and left.

With that, he left me alone to process what had just happened.

I heard the front door open. Mike was home.

I waited ten minutes. Then twenty. Then thirty. But no one came in to check on me or give me the usual lecture—about how they understood how difficult this was for me, how they were here for me. I had grown bored of hearing it, but deep down, it still felt nice. Almost like a way to hold onto the past.

It was odd. By this time, he would have usually come in to ask about me. But I guessed I had gone too far.

I could hear him talking to Brian in the other room, his voice hushed. I couldn't make out the words, but I could tell it was something serious. I thought he'd come to my room afterward. But he never did.

Then the thought hit me.

They wanted to replace me.

This was what my life would become—a constant movement from one home to the next. Until I turned eighteen. Then I'd have to figure things out alone.

I had no future. The people who had cared about me the most were gone. Now, I was just a burden to everyone else.

Unsure of what to do, I slipped on my thobe, put a kufi over my head, grabbed my prayer mat, and headed out the door to the nearest masjid.

This was the first time I had entered one since everything had happened.

The urge to go was impulsive, like I just needed to be in that vibe one final time.

I got there just in time for the Maghrib prayer. The imam started leading.

We were mid-prayer when it happened.

CHAPTER 5

There were five men. I barely remember what they looked like; the scene was all a blur. One of them took out a knife, another a gun. One even carried an axe, while another had pepper spray. All of them were armed with some sort of weapon, while I was only armed with Quranic verses.

I tried to focus on the salah, knowing that nothing could move me from prayer—that if I died, I wanted it to be in that moment. I closed my eyes for better concentration, but my heart was racing. I hadn't even reached the second sajdah when they began attacking everything and everyone around them.

Piercing screams. Random hateful phrases filled the room: *"Terrorists!" "You won't leave, so now we'll make you leave!" "Go back to your own country!"* A place of peace had turned into one of terror. They cursed, vandalized the mosque walls. The imam opened the emergency exit and ordered everyone out.

I began to run. A bullet grazed my arm—I touched it, and my fingers came away covered in blood. The pain was unbearable, but I kept running. Others were running too, fighting through the throbbing pain, running for their lives.

The prayer had been forgotten.

Guilt overwhelmed me. *I should have finished.* If I was meant to die, I should have at least died in sajdah. That would have guaranteed Jannah for me and my family. But now? Now I wasn't sure. Nothing was certain.

My mouth moved on its own, reciting a stream of prayers—verses from the Quran, duas I had heard my parents recite—anything and everything I could remember. I told myself that no matter what, I would end with shahadah.

My thobe was covered in dust, stained with blood. My kufi had blown off my head while I was running. Bodies littered the floor—some still clung to life, while others were just corpses.

I screamed when I saw the lifeless body of Mr. Hamid, an elderly man I had seen often at my apartment building. Someone's grandfather. A common masjid attendee. An uncle to all the youth. I barely knew him, but I was enraged.

I turned away, my stomach churning. His face was completely pale, arms sprawled around him.

I tried to keep running, but I froze. The gunfire still rang in my ears.

I stayed that way until a police officer came in and pulled me out.

Outside, chaos. A crowd had gathered in front of the masjid. Police cars. Ambulances. A fire truck. News reporters.

It became too much—the pain in my arm, the flashing lights, the noise.

I caught a glimpse of the attackers in handcuffs being led away by the police. Then, I collapsed. The hard concrete, covered in broken glass and blood, met me.

Everything went black.

When I woke up, my eyes met a blinding white light. It hurt to look at, so I closed them and escaped into the darkness.

But the darkness didn't last. Images flickered in and out. I didn't know if they were dreams or flashbacks.

In one, I was on the ground, covered in blood, a man pressing a knife against my throat.

In another, I was running toward a door, but with each step, it grew further away.

In another, I was running—and then I looked up.

Maryam was in the sky.

"Run," she told me. *"Don't look back."*

I opened my eyes again.

A hospital bed. A large bandage on my left arm. An IV in my right.

Mike and Brian stood beside me.

"He's awake!" Mike exclaimed.

"Are you alright, Muhammad? How do you feel?" Brian asked, his voice laced with panic.

"Fine. Just a little dizzy," I muttered. I tried to lift my arm, but a sharp pain shot through me.

"Ouch!" I hissed.

"The doctor said it may hurt for a while since the bullet grazed you deeply, but you're going to be alright," Mike reassured me. *"I'll let the doctor know you're awake. Just take it easy."*

My mind went straight to the masjid.

It had been the cause of my family's death. And now, this.

The masjid was supposed to be the house of Allah. It was supposed to be where I felt safest.

But now?

Now, I wasn't sure I could ever step inside one again.

As a first-generation Muslim American, I was not blind. I knew that Islamophobia was real. I just never thought it would happen to me with such severity. Ever since 9/11, hearing about masjids being attacked had become common. But I never thought I would be in one when it happened.

It was so unfair. Why did I have to deal with the hate and consequences of something that happened before I was even born? Why did people have to be so ignorant? And why did that ignorance have to fall on me? If they could just visit a masjid, they would see that Islam was a religion of peace, not violence.

Another wave of anger was about to hit me when I suddenly remembered—how one time, shortly after she started wearing the hijab, a boy in one of Maryam's classes pulled it off. She had come home crying, shaking in fear. I was ready to go find him and make him pay, but Mom stopped me. She sat both of us down and reminded us that even when Islam was first revealed, it wasn't accepted by everyone. The Prophet Muhammad, peace be upon him, endured hate and humiliation because of his beliefs. Despite this, he still loved those who hated him. He continued to pray for them, trying to show them the right way.

"You carry the name of the greatest man to ever live, Muhammad," she had said. *"Please lead by his example. If someone says something bad about Islam, show them the real Islam."*

The Prophet Muhammad faced religious persecution. The people of Palestine are still facing it today. And I—I was just one of many. The only difference between me and them was that I had a voice, and I intended to make it heard.

"How did you know I was here?" I asked, still dizzy. "How did you know what happened?"

"When you stormed out without saying anything, we were worried about you. But we figured you had probably gone to the masjid. Brian went after you, and when he saw what had

happened, he called me. I came running as fast as I could. I was the one who rode with you in the ambulance. You don't remember? You were moaning, asking for us, for your parents, for Maryam."

"I don't remember anything. Everything has been a blur since I fell."

"Never do anything like that again, Muhammad," he said, his tone firm now. *"The city is a dangerous place. Things like this happen. What if we hadn't thought to look for you at the masjid? The next time you want to go anywhere, you have to let me know."*

"I'm sorry," I said. *"I'm really sorry."*

He actually cared. Both of them did. They had all been genuinely worried about me. Maybe they were different. But I still couldn't be too sure.

When the doctor came in, he told us I would have to spend the night—they still needed to run some tests to make sure the fall hadn't affected my brain.

"Would one of you like to stay with him?" he asked.

"I was planning to go to the masjid and see if we could help in any way tonight," Mike said. *"But if you need me to stay, Muhammad, I will."*

"Just go. I'll be fine. That's more important right now. What happened to me has already happened." Then, I glanced at Brian. *"When you come back tomorrow, could you bring me the brown notebook on my desk? I need it."*

"Of course. But hopefully, you'll be out by then."

Soon after, Mike left, and only Brian remained. He hesitated before stepping closer.

"I'll stay with you, if you want."

"I'd like that. Thanks."

The chain that had held me back since I said goodbye to my family—the one keeping me from moving on—was starting to break. And for the first time, I could feel myself getting closer to the door.

A door to a potentially brighter future.

A door open to the formation of new friendships.

A door open to acceptance and adaptation.

Brian and I spent the rest of that night in an awkward silence. I was still wary of letting people get close to me. I wanted to apologize but didn't know how, and I wasn't sure if he was ready to accept it. He seemed distant, no longer as enthusiastic about getting to know me. For the most part, he ignored me.

While I went in for a couple of scans, Brian was on the phone with Mike, assuring him that I was alright and updating him on what the doctor had said. When I was done, we played *Roblox* together. It was funny how Brian was just like Maryam—he hated confrontation and went out of his way to put everyone at ease.

I, on the other hand, carried a constant rage within me. The car accident had only fueled it, but strangely, the shooting seemed to be calming it down. I tried to live by my name, to follow the teachings of the greatest man to walk this earth. Yet, that side of me—the part devoted to

Islam—was something I didn't always express with love and tenderness. Instead, I forced my identity upon people. Islam was supposed to be a religion of peace, but I was bitter and angry.

I implemented Islamic teachings into every aspect of my life but kept my guard up with everyone. In conversation, I was curt—not mean, just passive. But when provoked, I attacked mercilessly.

Being here in the hospital, though, had started to break through that hard outer layer of my heart. I could feel myself becoming more sensitive. Yes, it meant I was more vulnerable, but it also meant I could express my emotions freely. I could be more genuine, more open. Healing would take time and effort, but for the first time, I was willing to embrace it. More importantly, I was open to letting people be there for me.

I wanted them to be there for me.

But I knew I would have to earn that.

CHAPTER 6

The next morning, after a thorough examination, I was able to leave the hospital since my scans came out clear. Mike arrived to take me home. He told me that the masjid board had arranged for a cleanup the following weekend and that the city would be paying for the reconstruction.

I also learned that what had happened received a lot of media attention, as expected. But I knew it wouldn't last. It never does. This wasn't the first time something like this had happened. The commotion would fade in a few days. Civilians would move on with their lives, chasing the next big news story—while the victims of this shooting would remain scarred forever.

The thought angered me. So many lives had been changed, yet the nation still neglected us. This country calls itself the land of the free, but what kind of freedom is this if I have to leave my house each morning fearing for my life? Why do I have to live up to the expectations that society places upon me? Why must I conform to their double standards? Why am I expected to believe the lie that we are all equal when I know I am being treated as inferior?

If a Muslim gang or terrorist organization had gunned down a church, the country wouldn't get through it so easily. The media would go crazy. But when it's us, they choose to ignore it. Muslims have been oppressed for decades, suffering in silence while the world looks away. The war in Yemen gets no attention. The genocide in Palestine is labeled a war, and Palestinians—despite their pain and scars—are called the oppressors. And now here I am, facing my own struggle for the sake of my faith.

Jihad. Internal conflict.

Being a Muslim in the twenty-first century is becoming harder and harder. Doing my Islamic duty of giving *dawah* was never easy.

I recovered quickly. My physical wounds were healing, and soon, most would no longer be visible. But the emotional scars—those would remain etched into my heart forever. To this day, I still get nightmares about that dreadful night.

I knew I couldn't let that attack silence me. I had to do something. I had to speak out. But how?

I needed my voice to reach people worldwide. And so, I turned to YouTube.

I decided to make a video telling my story. I refused to let this be forgotten. I refused to let the world move on so easily. I wanted this attack to leave an imprint on society —the same way it had on me.

I borrowed Mike's camera, sat down in the living room, and began.

"Assalamualaikum."

Did that statement intimidate you? Disgust you in any way? Did you feel the need to turn off your screen the moment I said it?

It probably made you automatically identify me as a Muslim.

A Muslim—someone who lives their life in submission. Islam means submission. Muslims submit themselves to God and God alone. Is that really something to be afraid of? A religion that promotes peace and worship?

The greeting *assalamualaikum* means *peace be upon you.* So tell me—how is it that I wish peace upon you, and suddenly, you're afraid?

It's because you don't take the time to understand. You don't take the time to learn about the religion. To even know who we are.

My name is Muhammad Arshad, and I am one of the victims of the mosque shooting that took place last week.

Remember that?

I know it's been a while, and many of you have probably moved on with your lives.

I haven't.

I don't think I ever will.

My life has been forever changed by the cruel, heartless acts of those who dared to carry out such an attack. Believe me, I have known enough change, hardship, and loss over the past few months. I lost my parents and younger sister all at once. I had to leave the only home and life I had ever known. I had to adjust to a new family, a new routine—an entirely different existence.

That night, I went to the masjid searching for familiarity, hoping to escape the harsh reality I was living in.

But reality found me anyway.

I went there seeking the very thing that my religion stands for—peace. Instead, I faced the worst kind of violence imaginable. That night, I lost so much. I lost many people who, like me, belong to the Muslim community. I lost the sense of calm I feel when I enter the masjid. But what hurts the most is that I lost my trust in the American people.

I do not blame the shooters as much as I blame our government. I know that when many of you hear this, you'll just think, "Oh, another attack." This response highlights the unfortunate reality we live in—a reality where these kinds of attacks are just another part of American life. We've become so accustomed to violence that we no longer react.

We live in one of the greatest countries in the world. Why do we fail to tackle such an important problem? We need to take action.

I'm just a normal teen. I go to school, I like playing basketball, and I have big dreams for the future. Why do you see me as a threat? How can people be so ignorant as to stereotype an entire religion of over 1.9 billion followers because of the actions of a few individuals?

It is our job as Muslims to spread knowledge about Islam and its beauty. Islam is a religion of peace. Our goal is to live in peace and spread peace. Salaam means peace, and that is our mission. It is the responsibility of non-Muslims to begin recognizing Muslims as human beings and active members of society.

This was not the first attack, but perhaps we can make it the last.

I stopped recording, edited the video, and uploaded it immediately. That was my first step toward something greater. I didn't know where I was going or how big it would become. I just wanted to provoke some change.

I uploaded it in a sudden surge of rage and passion—a desire to make my voice heard, even if just a little. That video would end up changing everything from that day forward. My voice would be heard in ways I never expected.

CHAPTER 7

I never thought that one video could change so much, but it did. The video blew up overnight, and by the next morning, it had over a million views. My Instagram DMs and comments on other social media platforms flooded in, with people expressing their sympathy, saying they were sorry I had to go through that and that they'd stand by me no matter what I decided next. But the truth was, I didn't know what my next steps would be. I thought the video would be enough, but I guess it wasn't.

I decided to go to the place where it all started, hoping for some clarity. I asked Brian if he'd walk with me to the masjid, and he hesitantly agreed. We walked side by side in silence, but with each step, I felt something I hadn't before. It was as though I was walking with Maryam. The tension between us was melting away, and I was starting to feel closer to him than ever.

When we arrived, I was stunned by the progress. It looked as if the attack had never happened. It was even better than before. The structure seemed brand new, and people were entering the mosque to pray. I asked Brian if he wanted to join, and he agreed. Inside, I saw they were offering the Janazah prayers to honor the lives lost in the shooting. I took off my shoes and joined them while Brian lingered near the shoe rack.

I closed my eyes, immersing myself in the Imam's serene recitation of Surah Yaseen, silently following along in my head. When we prostrated in sujood, I prayed harder than I ever had before—praying for guidance, serenity, stronger faith, a deeper sense of purpose, and patience for whatever came next.

When the service ended, I prayed Isha—the night prayer—said salaam to everyone, and left.

Brian and I walked home, and as we reached our block, I saw my history teacher, Mr. Carter. He stared at me with such intense hatred that I winced and quickly looked away. His glare cut through me, leaving me in a haze of pain—though I couldn't tell if it was physical or mental. Then, he began walking toward me. I became terrified, instinctively backing away slowly, hoping he would sense my fear and stop. But he was oblivious. Each step he took only made my heart race faster.

When he reached us, he spoke, his voice as cold as ice, enunciating each syllable slowly. It pricked my skin and pierced my ears, hurting my heart in a way I hadn't expected. I clutched my chest, already feeling the weight of his words before he'd even finished. I wanted him to stop before he even started.

"I saw your video online. You are nothing, Muhammad. Nada. Nothing. All of you are. You come into this country, polluting it with your backwards ideologies, and then have the audacity to play the victims. Trust me, you'll get nowhere, and we'll make sure of that."

I shook my head, unable to understand. Then, my voice found its way out, despite the lump in my throat.

"We are what made this country what it is today. This nation is a nation of immigrants. What would be left if you removed every immigrant? And what makes you think you can do it alone? There's something called democracy. As a so-called history teacher, you'd think you'd understand that much."

I turned, and we walked away, the words hanging heavily in the air. How could one person remove every immigrant from a country as vast as the United States? It was clear he was just spreading false threats, but it still made me sick that someone—especially a teacher—could harbor such hatred for a specific group of people. What had we done to deserve it? And what did he mean by "we"? Who else was with him? What did he want?

There wasn't much he could do anyway, I thought. I was pretty sure it was illegal for anyone—especially a teacher—to talk to a student like that. Yet the fact that we weren't on school grounds, that he was an adult and I was still a teenager, scared me. His authority over me in that moment made me question how safe I really was. I couldn't shake the feeling that he wasn't the only one who felt this way.

My intention with the video was to raise awareness, not to instigate hatred, yet I managed to do just that. I hated the vulnerability I was drowning in. It had initially overwhelmed me when I first came to terms with the true meaning of the word *death*. I remember a whirlwind of words and emotions rushing through my body and mind. The mental and emotional battle I was thrown into was relentless. There was this sudden urge to exit my body, to witness the pain from a third-person perspective. I struggled to breathe and then, finally, collapsed to the floor, unable to stand, feeling a weight I couldn't describe. Darkness overtook me, lasting what felt like an eternity.

When I opened my eyes, one thought consumed me: *never*. Never again would I see my family. Never again would I trust anyone. Never again would I feel the true meaning of love. Never again would I experience such pain.

Standing alone with Brian, watching as Mr. Carter disappeared into the distance, I realized I was wrong. It wasn't "never again." I would be hurt. I would be hurt badly if I didn't figure things out. I didn't know what Mr. Carter was planning, but I knew I had to think quickly. I owed myself that much.

The encounter left me with constant pangs of fear and confusion that afternoon. I felt an urge to pull out my journal and write. I thought about how Allah tests each of His creations differently, and how the bigger the test, the stronger His love. I wanted to share Islam with the world, to portray my beliefs in the best possible light. But what was the point if I wasn't also going to serve the Ummah? What if my work meant ignoring the cries of my brothers and sisters?

Mr. Carter had hurt me, but that pain wasn't enough to silence me or make me comply with injustice beyond my own encounters with Islamophobia. I needed to reassess my priorities. I needed to implement my principles, not just share them. I wrote about the changes ahead and what they would require of me. I had to be real and raw, embracing my quirks and flaws. Doing so would allow me to build trust, to show that in addition to being a Muslim, I was also human. People like Mr. Carter especially needed to see that.

I wrote about Palestine. Western media was biased, sharing only what they wanted, while the Middle East had stories of its own—stories I needed to hear. Maryam and I grew up hearing about the Nakba from our parents. It always struck me as absurd how, in school, we learned about the Holocaust in great detail, going deep into its graphic atrocities. Yet, we were never taught about the sorrow that followed the end of World War II for the Palestinians. The lives lost, the families torn apart, the land stolen. Everyone condemned the Holocaust, but when it came to the Palestinian genocide, it was "complicated."

Zionism was condoned, while our people were forgotten—forgotten all over the world. Our tears gained no sympathy, our blood no commiseration, our screams no attention.

CHAPTER 8

The next day was a school day, and last night's encounter was still fresh on my mind as I slowly approached the subway station. I dreaded the first class I had that day. It took everything I had to put one foot in front of the other and drag myself to school. Every step felt like ten miles. Every second felt like an eternity. School was the last place I wanted to be. Yet, it was inevitable.

I approached the classroom slowly and hesitantly took my seat. I opened my bag quietly, as if the sound of the zipper unlatching would disturb the class—already full of restless adolescents who, like me, would rather be anywhere but school. Unlike me, though, they all had friends, huddling tightly in their own groups, taking advantage of Mr. Carter's obliviousness to catch up after the weekend.

I took out my notebook and pretended to be absorbed in taking notes, although, to be honest, I had no idea what he was saying. I just hoped he wouldn't notice me.

When class ended, I packed my things and rushed to get out, hoping he wouldn't see me, hoping I could somehow escape. Then, suddenly, he called my name.

"Muhammad, could you stay for a moment, please?"

"S-s-sure," I replied, immediately feeling my heart rate spike.

He waited for the classroom to clear out before he began.

"Don't forget what I said to you yesterday. You better watch your back around me, or I will make you regret it."

This time, instead of silently walking away, a sudden rush of anger filled me. I tried to conceal it, but it erupted. Like a pot of milk simmering for too long—screaming out, but nobody listening. Until it overflowed, and finally, people rushed to clean the mess.

Who did this guy think he was? How could he threaten to take me away from the only home I knew?

"You really think that YOU have the power to kick millions of people out of their country? Who do you think you are? How could you claim that you're a history teacher when you don't even know the rights that our founding fathers left for every citizen of this country? I'm an American citizen, and I know my rights. Many people lost their lives for me to attain them, and I will not let someone like you take them away. I think it's you who should watch your back around me because I will make you regret every word that comes out of your mouth."

With that, I left the classroom with a sense of triumph. I felt as if I had won a huge battle. But little did I know, the real battle was just beginning.

I found Sam waiting for me in the hallway, and we started walking to math class together.

"What did he want?" he asked.

I told him everything, starting from last night. He remained silent for a few seconds, processing the information, then finally muttered a simple, "Damn."

"I know, and I don't know what to do about it."

When we got to the classroom, I was met by a mob of kids. Everyone was hugging, congratulating me, and even wanting to take selfies.

"What's going on?" I asked, confused.

"Your video just hit over three million views on YouTube!" squealed Ali, a boy I didn't know very well but shared a few classes with.

I took out my phone to check YouTube, and sure enough, they were right. The video had reached 3,000,500 views and counting. I looked through the comments: one said, "Yay, Muhammad!" Another said, "Keep going! You've got this!" There were some not-so-great ones too, but I tried not to pay attention to those.

I was in shock. Completely overwhelmed. I still couldn't believe the shooting had happened, yet now things were changing—and fast.

Soon, the bell rang, and the excitement slowly began to die down. Everyone settled into their seats for class.

Before we dove into Precalc, my math teacher, Ms. Miller, said she needed to make an important announcement. I silently groaned—this usually meant a test the next day.

"I would like to start off our class today by congratulating one of our students on their efforts to speak out against an issue that unfortunately exists in our country. Excellent job, Muhammad. I encourage you to continue speaking out, and I apologize on behalf of this entire nation for the trauma that you and all of the other victims of that shooting endured. If you ever need anyone to talk to or assistance in any future action you may want to take, just know that we are here for you."

At that, everyone gave a round of applause. As the clapping slowly came to a conclusion, Ms. Miller announced there would be a test the next day.

Once school ended, I found Brian in front of the building, and we walked together toward the subway station. He tried to walk ahead of me and take another route, but I caught up with him and put a hand on his shoulder to stop him.

"I'm sorry, Brian," I said. "I'm really sorry, and I don't want you to say you forgive me just because your parents told you to. I truly want you to forgive me, and for us to be friends, but I get it if you don't want to. I don't want to use what I went through as an excuse for what I did. I have no excuse. All I can say is that I'm sorry."

He stopped walking. "Do you really mean that?" he asked.

I nodded. "You know, when you first came to stay with us, I was really excited. I thought I'd finally have someone like an older brother. Someone I could talk to and hang out with. I was so focused on what I had gained that I forgot to stop and think about what you lost and all you had to adjust to. I forgot that you needed space. I kept trying to force myself on you, trying to make you feel part of the family, but you weren't ready. You took it as me trying to replace your family, and I'm sorry for that too."

"Wow, that was deep. You sound just like—"

My voice trailed off. I hadn't spoken about Maryam to Brian before. I hadn't brought her up to anyone since her death, but at that moment, he reminded me so much of her.

"Like Maryam," I finished.

He hugged me, and for the first time, I hugged him back. "I'm sorry," I whispered.

On our walk to the train station, we started talking about the video.

"Did you see how many views I have now?" I asked him. "It was literally all anyone could talk about today."

When we got on the train, I was met by another mob. People recognized me and asked if I was the guy who was on the news and made that video. Apparently, when I had blacked out, cameras caught me being wheeled into an ambulance by the EMTs. My new "fans" began praising me for speaking out, telling me they were with me and to never stop fighting.

It was all so overwhelming that I was relieved when we reached our stop, eager to escape it all.

Brian unlocked the door to the apartment building, and we entered, greeted by Mike. He told me this was just the beginning. We had to think of something bigger to get the word out—something with a larger purpose.

I realized then that the video had reignited a passion in me that I thought had died out after I lost my family. It was a passion that had once been just a small glimmer, barely visible—a memory of something much bigger. But now it was bigger. Ten times bigger. Illuminating my heart, filling me with strength and motivation to keep moving forward.

That evening at dinner, all we could talk about was how much of a difference that video was going to make. The views kept climbing, and I was getting so much attention. Mike even said he wouldn't be surprised if it made it to the news. It certainly seemed possible, considering I had almost reached five hundred million views.

Before I went to bed that night, I decided to check the video one more time. When I opened the comments section, I was shaken. The nice, supportive comments I had seen earlier were now replaced with hateful, angry ones. Many came from people I knew—people from school and from back home in Pennsylvania.

Some of the comments were downright nasty. One claimed the whole shooting was a stunt to attract attention. Another was a death threat. It said that Muslims had no place in this country and that the person wouldn't rest until the creator of that video was dead. The account name was Mark Carter. Could that have been Mr. Carter? I didn't want to jump to conclusions, especially since I didn't even know his first name. But I felt a fear I had never experienced before.

I walked down the hallway to Mike's room and showed him my phone. Mike took a deep breath and said, "These comments were definitely expected, but don't let them discourage you. All of these threats are empty. They're from people who want to silence you. Don't give them that satisfaction."

"You're right. I should probably get to bed. Good night," I replied.

As I lay in bed that night, my mind raced with thoughts of what to do next. I wanted to find a way to honor the Muslims involved in the shooting, but I also wanted to honor Maryam and my parents. I got up, took out Maryam's journal, and turned to the last empty page. I started to write.

Dear Maryam,
I am confused. I am lost. Most of all, I am afraid. If you were

alive, I probably wouldn't be telling you this. I wouldn't want you to see me so vulnerable. As your older brother, I'm supposed to be the strong one. But ever since you died, I've never felt weaker. I need you to help me, support me, and guide me because I don't know what to do. I want to honor you, to make your legacy known, but you were always the one with the great ideas. I feel dumb for writing this, and for asking this, but Maryam, if you see this, please give me one more of your great ideas.

—Muhammad

I put the journal away and went to sleep, thinking about how much had changed and how much more would continue to change.

CHAPTER 9

The next day, I got ready for school with a nagging feeling in the pit of my stomach. I tried to fight it and carry on as usual, but it seemed to pull me back. The comments I had seen yesterday really scared me, and I had no idea what would happen next. I splashed some cold water on my face, trying to cool my growing anxiety, and focused more intently on my prayers.

Just before leaving, I grabbed Maryam's journal and the one Brian had given me, slipping both into my backpack for reassurance—something to rely on if everything went wrong. I changed the gauze on the arm the bullet had grazed. The injury, though small and minor, had changed so much. The emotional pain that accompanied it was excruciating, almost unbearable.

I forced myself to eat breakfast—bites of cereal and sips of orange juice. Then, I stood by the door, waiting for Brian to finish getting ready so we could leave. Once he was ready, I told him about the comments I had discovered last night and the bad feeling that weighed on me. He looked at me, concerned.

"Damn, bro, that's crazy," he said. "You have to be careful. The shooting and your video are gonna get a lot of attention, both good and bad. Be ready for the worst."

I thought the accident had made me tougher, that I could handle anything. But I realized I still needed to grow a thicker skin. I still needed to harden my heart and prepare for the worst. The accident had broken me down more than I thought—crushed and eroded my heart into pieces too small to put back together. I longed for reassurance that some part of me still felt alive, but that was gone. The people who had held my heart together were gone, too. What I showed on the outside was just a shell, a faint reflection of who I used to be, but could never be again.

Before hardening my heart, I knew I needed to rebuild it—nurture it, strengthen it, and comfort it. Then, I would lock it away, never allowing anyone to access its most intimate parts.

I got on the subway, sat down, and took out my history notes, trying to review for the day's lesson.

When we reached school, Brian and I said our good-byes and headed off to our separate first-period classes. I had Spanish first that day. Even though I had completed my foreign language requirement for high school graduation, I still loved the language and wanted to become fluent. The Spanish classroom was one of my favorites. My teacher, Mr. Martinez, made extra effort to keep it fun and colorful. Usually, I was excited for Spanish—it offered a glimpse into my old life. It let me forget, if only for a little while, and immerse myself in emotions that once defined me. But today, nothing could ease that bad feeling.

"Hola, Muhammad! ¿Qué te pasa?"

"Hola. I'm just overwhelmed, I guess. These past few weeks have been hard, and now with everything that happened last week, it's a lot to handle."

"I know it must be hard, and I can't even imagine what you've been through. But just know that I'm here if you ever need to talk. What you're doing is amazing, and don't let anyone tell you otherwise."

"Thanks, Mr. Martinez," I mumbled, genuinely grateful but still lacking the motivation or energy to maintain a steady, meaningful interaction.

I took a seat, pulled out my Spanish notebook, and prepared to start conjugating the verbs written on the board. Once I finished, I tuned out Mr. Martinez's voice and began writing in my journal. I wrote about random things—Maryam, Palestine, my friends in Pennsylvania. Anything and everything, but not once did I mention the shooting. I tried to keep it out of my mind for as long as I could.

The class flew by, and I didn't even realize the bell

had rung until I saw everyone packing up. I did the same and followed them out the door, dragging my feet to my next class. Dread overwhelmed my soul, spreading through my veins like venom, as cold as ice. I still wasn't sure if I should confront Mr. Carter about his comment. I decided against it. I didn't know how he would react, and I didn't want to find out. Instead, I decided I would talk to Mr. Martinez after school. He was the only teacher I truly trusted, and I knew he would listen.

I needed to talk, to blurt everything out, and watch an adult take charge for me. I needed someone to help me get through it and tell me that it's okay not to have all the answers, that I don't have to carry it all on my own. I texted Brian, telling him to wait for me in front of Mr. Martinez's room after school. Then, I entered the classroom and noticed the textbooks on each desk.

I quickly walked to my desk, sat down, and the class began. It went well, except for the occasional glare from Mr. Carter across the room, like he wanted to crush every bone in my body with just his bare hands. I ignored him and focused on the lesson as usual. When the bell rang, I swung my backpack over my shoulder and quickly left the room, careful not to make eye contact with him. I didn't want to know what would come next.

That day seemed to stretch on forever, class after class, lesson after lesson. I was tired of people asking how I was, but eventually, the day came to an end. After my last class, I made my way to Mr. Martinez's room. Fortunately, he was still there.

"Hola, Muhammad! What can I do for you?" he asked warmly.

"I need to talk to you about something. To be honest, I don't know who else to turn to."

"Sí, of course! What do you need?"

"It's about Mr. Carter. Ever since the attack, and even before that, he's been treating me really coldly." I told him about what happened when Mr. Carter encountered me and Brian, how he asked me to stay after class, and what he said to me then.

"Honey, you should have told somebody right away. It is illegal for a teacher to treat a student that way. He should be fired."

"There's also something else, although I don't want to accuse him without any proof. A while after my video went viral, I came across a comment that was a death threat against me. The person who sent it was named Mark Carter. I suspected it was him, though I don't know his first name, and I don't think he would go that far."

I showed her the comment on my phone, and she observed it silently.

"His first name is Daniel, so it's unlikely that it's him. Even so, what he did to you was wrong, and we need to talk to Mr. Garcia about it. I also suggest you discuss the comment with your parents so you can figure out what to do."

"My parents died a few months ago. That's why I moved here. I'm living with a foster family for now."

"I'm so sorry to hear that. Do you feel comfortable talking to your foster family about it? If not, we can work something out."

"Thank you, and yeah, I already talked to them."

"That's good. I'll talk to Mr. Garcia, but I need you to email me a screenshot of the comment so I can show it to him, and we can determine whether or not it really was Mr. Carter."

"I'll do that right now. I don't know how to thank you, Mr. Martinez."

"There's no need to thank me. I'm just glad you came to me."

I left the room much calmer than I had been when I entered.

CHAPTER 10

I went home with a great sense of relief overwhelming me. The burden I had carried for so long was slowly lifting. The chains that had held me hostage, a prisoner to my own mind, were finally breaking away.

When I entered the apartment, I noticed the TV was on, and Mike was seated in front of it, watching the news. "15-year-old Muhammad Arshad, a sophomore at Willow Heights High School and one of the survivors of the tragic mosque shooting, went viral after deciding to speak out about what happened on YouTube. The teenager now has over six million views, all in just a few days."

I was in shock. If this managed to make it into the news, what would be next? Interviews? Articles? Things were moving so fast.

Upon seeing me, Mike immediately pulled me into a hug and told me how proud he was.

Later that evening, the idea hit me, an idea that would forever change my life — and the lives of many others — for the better. It came like an overwhelming epiphany, flooding my mind with clarity, like the sun breaking through after a long thunderstorm. It felt like light and clarity after a period of darkness.

I knew what I had to do to honor my family and those who died in the shooting while spreading the true meaning of Islam. I remembered how Maryam had talked about wanting to start a branch of the MSA (Muslim Students Association) at our school. She was so passionate about Islam, despite our town's relatively small Muslim community. Maryam was always at halaqahs, town hall meetings, school assemblies — sharing whatever knowledge she could about our religion.

I decided to do something similar, but bigger. A way to share Islam with the world. It would be called SALAAM. — Support And, Love And, Accept Muslims.

I would also create a YouTube channel for the organization to gain some level of fame. In it, I would share what happened during the shooting, as well as the stories of Maryam and my parents. I would educate people about Islam through stories and examples from the Quran. I could even do Quranic recitations with English translations, so that people could understand the words.

SALAAM would be more than just a YouTube channel. It would be a club where people of all ages could join, socialize, have fun, and learn about Islam. I would create a slideshow explaining SALAAM and sharing my story to show at school.

I had so many ideas, and they were coming so fast that I had to organize them. Thoughts kept bombarding me, one after another. I raced to my room, grabbed my journal, and began jotting down ideas.

I knocked on Brian's door and entered. I sat down on his bed and explained my idea to him. He was just as excited as I was and couldn't wait to get started.

"The mosque has a new spare room. We can ask the imam if we can meet there," he exclaimed. He blurted out idea after idea, getting all animated, just like Maryam would. He was speaking so quickly that my hand hurt from trying to write it all down.

"I'm going to start sketching out the brochure and get it to you by tomorrow. Then we can ask Dad to make more copies at his office. They have a copy machine there."

"Thanks, Brian. While you do that, I'll work on the second YouTube video explaining everything. The first one was too blunt and out of nowhere. If we're going to follow through, we need proper structure."

I borrowed Mike's camera and filmed another video, thanking everyone for their support on the first one and explaining the plan for the channel moving forward. I also included an email I created in case anyone had any questions. Additionally, I shared information about SALAAM, inviting everyone to join. When I finished recording, I edited the video and quickly uploaded it to my channel. Once that was done, I took out my books, sat down at my desk, and started my homework.

The next day was Thursday, the first day of Sha'ban, the eighth month in the Islamic calendar. My family and I always fasted a lot during Sha'ban to prepare for the following month—Ramadan. I couldn't believe this would be my first Ramadan without my family. I closed my eyes and remembered how, once a week during Ramadan, my parents would invite all of our neighbors, both Muslims and non-Muslims, over for iftar. I remember the nights before, spent cooking and laughing together. My mom was Moroccan, and my dad was Pakistani, so we often found ourselves blending both cuisines. We'd have tagine alongside biryani, drink Moroccan mint tea alongside Pakistani chai. Every meal was a fusion—something Arab and something South Asian.

I longed for those simple gatherings, the comfort of having everyone around me, and the simplicity that Ramadan used to bring. The purity found in that Holy month—the desire for self-improvement, self-forgiveness, and community unity—was something I looked forward to each year. Would it be the same this year? Would it ever be the same again? I longed for another month of submission, reflection, devotion, and, most importantly, connection—connection with the people who mattered most, the people I would never see again.

I decided to fast that day in an attempt to revive those memories. It also sparked an idea for SALAAM. Once a week during Ramadan, I would host iftar at the masjid. I wanted to fill the void in my heart while enriching the lives of my community. I could find people to sponsor the event or ask everyone to contribute one dish. It would be more than just a meal—there would be games for the kids and social hours for adults. While the Muslims went off to pray Maghrib, Isha, and Taraweeh, the non-Muslims could watch to better understand our customs. Members of SALAAM would spread the word about Islam's morals, helping society become more aware and accepting of our religion.

I woke up at 3:30 for Suhoor, the pre-dawn meal that would sustain me through the day. Stumbling down the hallway to the kitchen, I made myself a bowl of cereal and grabbed a banana from the fruit bowl. I ate, drank some water, and prayed Fajr—the first prayer of the day. I read some Quran, flipping to Surah Maryam. The chapter is dedicated to the greatest woman to ever live, the woman my sister was named after. The eloquence and perfection of each verse made me smile every time I read it.

CHAPTER 11

The morning dragged on slowly. My classes were constantly interrupted by teachers stopping by to see if I was "that kid from the news." Yeah, I was—but I was more than that. I was Muhammad, and I didn't want my name and identity to be forgotten just because the media had captured one moment of my life.

People seemed more interested in the fact that I had been on the news than in why I had been on the news. It felt like I was turning into some kind of celebrity at school. I wasn't sure how I felt about the fame. I was hurting, and so were many others. The world was full of prejudice and injustice, yet all anyone seemed to care about was my face on TV.

At lunch, I met up with Brian. He handed me an envelope with the brochure inside, then raced off to his next class. I sat down at one of the computers and opened it.

I was amazed. The design had been done by hand and then scanned onto the computer. The lettering was simple but unique. The front read: "SALAAM MEANS PEACE." Below it, each letter of SALAAM was spelled out with its meaning.

The back featured a dedication:

"In loving memory of Hassan, Sara, and Maryam Arshad."

Beneath it was a picture of Maryam, smiling in a flowing pink dress—the same picture I kept on my desk. Below that was a photo of my parents right after their wedding. They looked so young and full of ambition. Their eyes shone with life and passion, and years of marriage hadn't changed that. Maryam and I would catch them glancing at each other the same way they did in that photo, and we'd smile.

I had always made dua, hoping Allah would one day grant me a marriage like theirs.

At the bottom of the page, there was a small paragraph I had written:

"Who would have known that a trip to the mosque would lead to three lives being ended? I lost my mom, dad, and sister all in one night, and ever since then, my life has never been the same. Every night, I go to bed wondering why they died while I lived. I grew up believing that God has a reason for everything. Their deaths had a purpose—a test to see if I would let my faith waver. My survival had a purpose, too: to share their

story and share Islam with the world. SALAAM allows me to do both."

Inside, the brochure contained a description of my channel, details about the shooting, and information about the club—where we would meet and what we would be doing. I had also included an email address I created last night for any questions or concerns.

Holding the brochure in my hand made everything feel real. I was actually making this happen. But none of it would have been possible without Brian or Maryam—and none of it would continue unless Mike approved.

I quickly put together a slideshow, adding similar information from the brochure. Just as I finished, the bell rang. I rushed off to my afternoon classes.

History was right after lunch, and I was nervous about seeing Mr. Carter after telling Ms. Martinez what he had done to me. To my surprise, he wasn't there. Instead, Mr. Garcia stood at the front of the room.

"Class, due to some complaints we received, Mr. Carter will no longer be teaching your class," he announced. "Ms. Martinez has a prep period, so she'll substitute today while we find a long-term replacement."

A huge weight lifted off my shoulders. I would never have to see Daniel Carter again.

When the day finally ended, Brian and I met in front of the school. I couldn't stop thanking him and going on about how professional the brochure looked. No one would believe a high schooler had made it.

"You should seriously consider going into graphic design," I told him.

But Brian just laughed. "I've got my heart set on engineering."

At the subway station, we were once again met by a mob of people.

"Bruh, I thought my fifteen minutes of fame would be over by now," I whispered to Brian.

He laughed.

After countless congratulations, good lucks, thank yous, and selfies, we finally escaped the crowd and got onto our train.

There, I turned to Brian. "I want you to be my social media manager," I said. "Only if you want to. You'd be working for free for now since this is a non-profit organization."

Brian didn't even hesitate.

"Of course, I want to."

We rode in silence for a while, and my old worries started creeping back. Just as I was finally making my way toward the door—trying to escape the dark room I had been shackled in since losing my family—the thought of losing my foster family made the chains I had broken trap me once again. They clutched my heart mercilessly, refusing to let me gasp for air.

I had not exactly been nice to them in the beginning.

What if they had complained to my social worker? What if the agency decided to place me in another home? What if it was so far away that I'd never see Mike or Brian again? What was the point of going through SALAAM if I would only have to leave in the end? The more I thought about it, the more I began to question if it was a great idea at all. Maybe it wasn't. Maybe I needed to stop all of this.

Once we arrived, I was appalled at what I discovered.

I entered the apartment and greeted Mike, who was home early from work, preparing dinner—which, for me, would be iftar. I headed down the hall to my room to change, as usual. Slipping into a pair of shorts and a T-shirt, I sat at my desk and quickly checked the email account I had created for SALAAM. There was one new message.

I opened it.

It was from *The Tonight Show*. They had heard about my videos and wanted to interview me—two weeks from Saturday!

Heart pounding, I sprinted across the hallway to tell Brian. We both bolted to the kitchen to tell Mike.

"No wayyyyy!!!! Muhammad, that's AMAZING!"

All three of us were laughing and screaming. It felt surreal. The doubts that had consumed me on the subway vanished. I was going to put everything I had into SALAAM.

Brian and I spent the rest of the evening explaining

our vision to Mike. We played the slideshow for him and showed him Brian's brochure. He promised to make copies.

"The theme should be blue, right?" he asked.

"Yeah, with a black border," I replied.

We were so engrossed in planning that I didn't realize it was time for iftar until I heard the adhan (call to prayer) on my phone. That night, I went to bed happier than I had been in a long time.

As I passed the hallway on my way to my room, I heard Brian and Mike talking in hushed voices. For a moment, I considered joining them but decided against it. I climbed into bed, attempting to sleep, but I was too excited. Everything was happening so fast—it was over-whelming.

I got up, grabbed a pen and the journal Brian had given me, and began writing about everything that had happened in the past few weeks. I fell asleep with the book still in my hand and didn't wake up until morning.

The next two weeks were filled with making SALAAM a reality.

I spoke to Sheikh Omar, who loved the idea. Together, we made plans for Ramadan and decided that Friday would be the best day to host our meetings—it was the start of the weekend, after all. Brian and I passed out copies of the brochure at school. He even posted a picture on Instagram. Then, he designed a flyer with the mosque's address and meeting times to make it easier for people to find us.

Before I knew it, the night before the interview had arrived.

The interview was scheduled for 11 AM. I hadn't told anyone at school about it—not even Sam, who was quickly becoming a close friend. When I finally called him, he was shocked. I apologized for not telling him sooner and asked him to tune in to the show.

The next morning, we rode to the TV station.

I put on a pair of jeans and a nice shirt. Standing in front of the mirror, I thought I looked ready to be on TV —though I certainly didn't *feel* ready. I searched for small amounts of confidence within me, praying it would be enough to hold me together. To strengthen me somehow. Yet, I was finding it hard to breathe.

Everything felt surreal—like this wasn't really happening.

But it *was.*

One way or another, I had to step into that studio and make an impact. I had to make a change. The attackers thought their guns were the most powerful weapons, but they were wrong.

Words are the most powerful weapon.

I want my words to penetrate through the skin and rest in the heart. I want my words to stay in a person's mind for a lifetime. I want my words to be the catalyst for something beautiful. When the right words reach the right audience, their impact can be unimaginable.

CHAPTER 12

The drive to the station was not long, and the three of us were mostly silent. Upon our arrival, anxiety gripped me. The whole world would see this. I wanted to be honest without oversharing. I wanted to start off on the right foot—there would be no do-over.

We were greeted by the host, Savannah Gurie.

"It's so great to have you guys here," she said with a bright smile. She was enthusiastic, telling me how honored she was to meet me and how grateful she was that I had agreed to be on the show. She offered us some snacks, but I was too nervous to eat.

"At least drink some water—you look really nervous."

I took the water bottle she offered and thanked her.

She led us backstage to a room with a clear view of the studio. "We'll be going live in five minutes," she said. "I'll call you in, so listen for my cue."

Mike and Brian would be watching from backstage, with the best view of everything. As the show was about to begin, I turned to Brian and confessed, "Bruh, I don't even know what I'm doing here."

"You're here to tell your story, and everyone wants to hear it." He smiled and gave me a gentle push forward.

"…Imagine losing your entire family, being injured in a shooting, enduring unimaginable levels of discrimination simply because of your religion—and channeling all of that fear, grief, and anger into a project that will benefit many. This is exactly what one teenager did. Everyone, please welcome 15-year-old Muhammad Arshad."

A round of applause erupted as I walked onto the stage.

"Thank you so much for joining us today, Muhammad," Samantha began.

"Thank you for having me. I'm glad to be here."

"Tell me, how has this past year been for you?"

I paused. I wanted to be honest, but I wasn't ready to share my entire life story with the world.

"It's definitely been hard," I said. "As you can probably imagine, losing your entire family—especially at such a young age—is difficult. I was constantly in fear of what tomorrow would bring, and I expressed that fear as anger. I hurt a lot of people without meaning to. All of that rage was rooted in the uncertainty of my situation, the unfairness of my circumstances, and the injustices I faced as a first-generation Muslim American. I would like to extend an apology to anyone I may have negatively impacted."

"You've been through a lot at your age, and a reaction is expected," she said. "The level of maturity you've shown by apologizing live on camera is outstanding. You truly are an amazing young man, Muhammad."

"Thank you so much."

"You'll have to face the shooters in court later on. How do you feel about that?"

"The trial won't be happening for a long time. I'm a little nervous—I'm not great with confrontation—but when the time comes, I think I'll be ready."

Another round of applause.

"The video you made after the shooting touched the hearts of many. What drove you to create it? And did you expect the amount of attention it received?"

This time, I knew exactly how to respond.

"Well, first of all, I definitely wasn't expecting this much attention. I made the video so people could see what the shooting meant to someone who actually lived through it. I wanted to open their eyes to the reality of being a Muslim in the United States at a time like this."

"Well, you clearly did just that. In your second video, you mentioned a project called SALAAM. Could you explain what you intend to do with it?"

"After my family died, I wanted to find a way to honor them, especially my sister Maryam. She was my best friend, someone I could always count on for her great ideas. When she died, she was still so young and full of life. As you can imagine, I was devastated.

Then, after the shooting, I felt an even stronger need to honor the lives lost and to portray my religion in a positive light. My mom had always taught me that if someone says something bad about Islam, the best response is to show them the real Islam. I struggled to find a way to bring all these things together, so I asked myself: *What would Maryam do?*

I then remembered how, before she died, she wanted to start a Muslim Student Association at our school. That gave me the idea for SALAAM. But I didn't want it to be just for students—I wanted it to be a place where people of all ages, religions, and backgrounds could come together, have fun, learn about Islam, and hopefully become more accepting of it.

I still have a long way to go—I only just got approval for our meeting location—but I hope to make this a reality."

"Well, if there's anyone who could do it, it's definitely you, Muhammad. We wish you the best of luck."

There was another round of applause.

"We're now going to move on to some more personal questions about your life at home. If there's anything you're not comfortable answering, you don't have to."

"Okay, sure."

"After everything you've been through, do you still consider yourself a normal teenager?"

"Well, everyone has a different definition of normal, but I think I would. Like most of my peers, I enjoy hanging out with my friends, playing basketball, and listening to music. However, unlike some other teens, there are certain things I don't do because they're not permissible in my religion.

Sometimes, I reflect on everything I've been through and realize how much I've changed. I wonder if others have faced similar struggles. Then I remind myself that everyone has their own share of problems—and that, too, is just a part of being normal."

"Wow, you're such an intelligent young man—wise beyond your years."

"Thank you so much."

"Could you describe your relationship with your foster family?"

"My foster family and I are really close, especially my foster brother, Brian.

When they first took me in almost eight months ago, I was still in shock, and I took that out on them. But we've moved past that. Now, I've even started thinking of them as just *my* family. I love them. And knowing that I won't be with them forever is something that weighs on me every day.

For a long time, I hesitated to tell them how I felt. I was afraid they might not feel the same way."

I paused. I realized I had said too much.

"Well, we hope everything works out. Now, we actually have a surprise for you to wrap up this interview. If you could just follow me right this way."

I got up and followed them to a spot in front of a white curtain. What could it be? A gift card? A college scholarship? I thought of all the typical talk-show giveaways and wondered if one of them was meant for me.

"Now," said Hoda, "I want you to stand here, and I'll pull up the curtain to reveal your surprise."

I stayed put as Hoda and Samantha backed away. The curtain lifted.

Mike and Brian stood there, smiling.

For a moment, I was confused. Then, I saw the sign Brian was holding:

You were chosen. You are wanted. You are cherished. You grew in our hearts. You are the missing piece. Welcome to the family.

I froze. Could this mean what I thought it did? My legs felt locked in place as I stared at them, my mind racing.

"Is it true? Are you sure? Do you... do you really mean it?"

Mike nodded. "Only if you want to," he said gently. "We won't force anything on you. You can keep your last name, continue practicing your religion, and embrace your culture. We don't want to erase your past, but we hope to be part of your future."

Brian stepped forward. "We can't replace your real family," he said, "but hopefully, we can make a difference in your life."

Emotion surged through me. I ran to Brian and threw my arms around him. "You are my family," I whispered. "You're my brother." Then I turned to Mike, hugging him just as tightly. "Thank you," I whispered, my throat tight with emotion.

Confetti burst around us, raining down in a swirl of color. But no gift card or college scholarship could compare to this moment.

For the first time in a long time, I felt like I was one step closer to a forever home.

For the first time in a long time, I felt free.

And I was more determined than ever to keep moving forward.

CHAPTER 13

"How did you pull it off? What made you decide? Why me? I'm a teenager—I'll be 16 in a few months. Wouldn't you have wanted someone younger?"

It was the next day. The four of us were in the kitchen, eating breakfast and discussing last night's events.

"Do you remember the night of the shooting?" Brian asked. "The night when you snapped at me?"

I nodded, cringing at the memory.

"Well, that was the night we decided," Mike said. "Brian told us what you said to him, and we realized that you needed help. You needed a permanent home and some stability in your life. We knew we could provide you with that. And so we began the process."

Later that night, I began to wonder how my life would look from now on. I was almost sixteen. In two years, I would be an adult. I had to figure out what to do with my life.

I was lucky—fortunate enough to have a family that would help me through it all. My mind went back to the night when everything had changed. Almost seven months had passed since then. In some ways, it felt like merely seven days; in others, it felt like seven years.

I remembered how helpless and vulnerable I had felt, like I had no control over anything. I remembered how long it took for me to accept Mike as my guardian, how long it took to adjust to life without my family—and to accept that I would never fully adjust. I remembered how much I struggled to continue practicing my religion while living with non-Muslims.

As much as I would give anything to have my family back, I would not change all that I had experienced. The hardship, the joy, the loss, the suffering, the homesickness. All of these shaped me into who I was today.

There was a court hearing to make things official. It was all a blur. I barely remembered anything from it, except for Mike and Allison signing a few papers and the judge saying a few words. But when we came home, I finally started to feel like I belonged—like I was part of the family.

One night, as I lay in bed, I started thinking about SALAAM and the purpose it would fulfill.

I was blessed while so many others weren't. I had been given a second chance at life, a second family, and a platform to give dawah—a way to honor the family I had lost. I wanted to use the attention I was getting to raise awareness. Not just for myself, but for my community as a whole.

I got out of bed and fell to the floor in **sajdah**. I needed to talk to Allah. I needed to seek His guidance.

When we prostrate on the ground, Muslims are closest to their Creator. In order to gain acceptance for my people, I needed to learn about them. I needed to immerse myself in their struggles, clear any misconceptions, and aid them when they needed it.

We are taught that the Muslim community worldwide is called the **Ummah** of Prophet Muhammad. The **Ummah** is one body. When one part hurts, the entire body hurts. When one part bleeds, the entire body bleeds. When one part cries, the entire body cries. We lean on one another in times of need, and we uplift one another in times of sorrow.

My community had uplifted me in my times of need. Now, I needed to reciprocate that.

SALAAM couldn't just be about educating people about Islam or telling others to support Muslims. It needed to actually provide the support necessary.

CHAPTER 14

The last couple of weeks leading up to Ramadan were hectic. My friends from Ridgmore started reaching out, asking how I had been, about the shooting, and about SALAAM—including Ahmad. I hadn't spoken to him since the move, so we spent an hour catching up through text. I apologized for not reaching out sooner, but he told me he knew I had been going through a lot and just wanted to make sure I was okay.

That's the thing with best friends—it didn't matter whether you went three hours or three years without speaking, you could always pick up right where you left off.

He asked me about the details of SALAAM, and I told him what I could, although I was still trying to figure things out myself.

"I missed you so much, bro. Seeing you in pain like that hurt all of us too, wallah. My mom asks about you every day."

"I miss you guys too. I'm so sorry for losing contact. I won't do that ever again, bro, I promise."

Between school, SALAAM, and all the attention from the interview, I barely had a moment to breathe. I couldn't go from one class to the next without someone congratulating me or asking for a photo. I used my newfound recognition as an opportunity to advertise SALAAM.

Our first meeting was set for the first night of Ramadan, which would fall on a Saturday this year. I talked to Sheikh Omar about getting a few long tables and chairs.

"Don't worry, the masjid has plenty of those—we got you," he said excitedly. He was just as ready as we were.

I planned to pay for a projector out of pocket, with some help from Mike. I also needed to put together a speech to go along with the presentations. For the first meeting—and all of the meetings held during Ramadan—iftar would be served. Sheikh Omar assured me that the masjid would cover the cost of the first night's meal, catered by a Middle Eastern restaurant nearby. Mr. Martinez, who said he would attend, even offered to bring cupcakes.

On the website Sam had made, I made sure to mention that anyone was welcome to bring food to share. We created a Google Form to get a headcount, and within the first hour, forty people had signed up. We had to cap attendance at seventy-five. We made it clear that access to meetings would be on a first-come, first-served basis. Later, we would have a signup sheet for attendees to take turns bringing snacks.

Our meetings were scheduled an hour before Maghrib and would continue until Isha. Afterward, everyone was free to leave, but Muslims were welcome to stay for Taraweeh—the nightly prayer during Ramadan—and Suhoor. To enter the masjid, we asked everyone to dress modestly to a reasonable extent. The hijab was welcome and encouraged but not mandatory for non-Muslims. While one goal of this club was to teach people about Islam, the bigger purpose was for everyone to learn about each other. I didn't want it to feel like we were trying to impose anything on anyone.

The day of our first club meeting, my family and I arrived at the masjid early to help set up.

"Brian, I'm going to get the chairs from upstairs. In the meantime, can you grab the tablecloths from the closet? And Mike, can you set up the projector?"

"Of course, go on."

I ran upstairs, dragging dozens of chairs into the elevator—only to get stuck in it.

Panicking, I pressed the emergency button. Nothing.

I shifted my weight against the chairs to keep them from toppling over. *Ya Allah,* I thought. *It's only the first day.*

I quickly called Sheikh Omar, who was able to force the door open.

"Dude, next time, don't overload the elevator. And you can always ask for help, you know."

"Yeah, but that takes too much time."

"Slow down," he laughed, shaking his head.

Mike and Brian had joined me in fasting for the day, and they looked eager for it to be over. Brian was wearing one of my thobes, and he looked really good in it. Mike had also slipped a Kufi on top of his head. I loved how they were making an effort to learn about Islam—always asking me questions and including themselves. It kind of made me feel less alone.

Sheikh Omar and I started setting up the tables. Brian joined us, unfolding them and placing a chair at each spot. The buffet table was set up in the back, and Mike was stacking paper plates, napkins, plastic forks, and cups on one side. I joined him, adding bottles of soda and juice.

"This looks really nice," he commented. "Hopefully, we can do it more often."

Shortly after we finished, people began to arrive. Sam came first, carrying a tray.

"S-Salaam," he said.

I laughed. "Salaam! Thanks for coming."

More guests arrived—some I knew, some I didn't. There were people from Mike and Allison's church, regulars from the mosque, and even family members of Mr.

Hamid. Some classmates from school came, including Aaliyah, a girl from my math class.

"Ramadan Mubarak!" she exclaimed. "This is amazing, Muhammad!" She handed me an aluminum tray. "I made samosas."

Ms. Martinez also arrived with her husband and kids.

"I don't know if I'm supposed to do this," she said, "but I really want to see how this goes."

"I'm glad you're here," I replied.

As soon as everyone arrived, the adhan went off—it was time to break our fast. I went around with Brian, Sheikh Omar, and a few regular masjid volunteers, handing out dates and water bottles.

After breaking our fast, it was time for Maghrib prayer. The women went upstairs while the men went to another room downstairs. Those who weren't comfortable praying were welcome to wait in the meeting room, though most were curious and made their way into the prayer hall.

Once we finished, everyone lined up to fill their plates. Despite fasting all day, I wasn't very hungry. Or maybe I was just nervous about how everything would go. I broke my fast with a sip of water and began circulating the room. I had never organized something this big before.

After dinner and cleanup, it was time for my presentation. I set up the projector and began my slideshow. People seemed to like it, excitedly shouting out ideas—

Quran competitions, games for younger kids, childcare, and study circles. These were all things that would be new to the mosque.

When the presentation ended, people naturally formed small groups. The adults sipped tea and chatted in one corner. The kids played Uno at a table. The teens huddled around me, telling me how impressive everything was and offering to help in any way.

Then Sam made a joke.

"All of this might just make me convert to Islam."

I could sense that some of the Muslims in the group were annoyed. So was I. But I just laughed it off and tried to keep the conversation going.

Ali, however, wasn't having it.

"Look," he said, crossing his arms. "No one's trying to convert anyone. If you like it here, great—you're welcome to stay. If you don't, then you're more than welcome to get the hell outta here."

"Dude, language! You're in the house of Allah," I retorted.

"Alright, then that's what I'll do. I don't stay where I'm not wanted."

With that, Sam turned to leave.

"Bro, come on, Ali," Brian said, going after Sam. "He was just joking. I get it, maybe he shouldn't have said that, but still, you were a little harsh."

Brian managed to persuade Sam to come back.

After a couple of apologies from both sides, everyone

started to calm down, and everything went smoothly afterward. As the night wore on, people began to leave. Most Muslims, however, stayed since, during Ramadan, we spend most of the night in worship.

Once everyone had left, Ali caught up with me.

"Tonight was really great, Muhammad," he began. "I'm sorry for the way I reacted to Sam's comment. It's just that after what happened at the masjid and how you spoke out, it finally felt like we were actually getting somewhere with tackling Islamophobia. And then it felt like Sam was trying to take that away. I can forgive a lot of things, but Islam is where I draw the line. I think you feel the same way."

"Sam's a good guy. He and Brian were the ones who helped me with all of this. Wallah, I could not have done it without them. They aren't even Muslim, but they're so enthusiastic about the organization—it amazes me. I know what he said was wrong, but I also know he only meant it as a joke."

"Well, I definitely see that now. Is there anything I could do to help? I would love to join your team."

"Well, Brian is managing my social media, and Sam is taking care of the website. I know we'll need more help down the line, and as soon as I figure out what else needs to get done, I'll let you know."

"Thanks, Muhammad. I'll see you on Monday."

"Yeah, later. Salaam!"

With that, he left to join his family outside, and I sat

down with my Quran for a night of reading. Its familiar words brought me comfort. Many things could change, but the Quran never would. Every Ramadan, I strove to complete it, and this one would be no different. Despite all the changes I had to adapt to this month, I still had my Quran, and that would never change.

The next day, I pulled out the journal Brian had given me and sat down at my desk to brainstorm ideas for SALAAM. I made a list of staff members and wrote down: Muhammad, Brian, Sam, and Ali. I thought Ali would make a great event organizer—he always had amazing ideas. Even in class, he never shut up.

I texted him to see if he was on board, and within ten minutes, he sent me a list of event ideas. I knew I had picked the right person for the job.

A while later, I put together a quick video using footage from last night and posted it on YouTube to update everyone on SALAAM. My subscriber count was climbing fast. Old friends started reaching out to check in on me. Catching up was nice, but when they asked how I was coping and reminisced about how we used to hang out, stressing over tests and homework, it reminded me of my old life—the life that had been taken away from me. A life I would never get back.

I never imagined that the accident and the shooting would take me this far, yet deep down, I was still lost and confused.

After an hour or so of brainstorming, I started feeling

hungry and headed to the kitchen for a snack. Just as I reached for an apple, I realized I was fasting. I groaned and went back to my room—iftar was only two hours away. I'd survive until then.

I put my journal away and studied for a bit since I had some upcoming tests. I pored over my physics textbook, trying to convince myself that understanding projectile motion and Newton's three laws was actually beneficial to my future. Ya Allah.

Once I was done, I took out my Quran and began reading until, at last, it was time for Maghrib.

By the time the sun set, I was starving. I sat down and ate. I don't remember what I ate—just that I ate, thinking of nothing but finishing quickly so I could get back to reading the Quran. Being able to understand its words gave me the sensation that it was speaking to me, making me long for more.

When I was finished, I prayed Maghrib and sat down to read some more. This had been my Ramadan routine ever since I learned how to read Arabic. Even before then, I would sit beside my parents with an open Arabic reader, attempting to decipher the words and their meanings, which remained a secret to me. Unlocking them always felt like a great accomplishment.

Being able to read in two languages gave me the ability to think in two ways, understand different cultures, and move between them seamlessly. I could access different interpretations and further appreciate the gift of language.

Later, I took out my phone and scrolled through the list Ali had given me. One idea stood out—an interfaith Eid carnival where people of all backgrounds could come together and celebrate. It was great in theory, but raising the money would take forever. Ali had already thought of that. He suggested a bake sale on Friday during the meetings. People would want desserts after iftar, and the options were always limited.

My goal for SALAAM surfaced in my mind again. I needed to work toward a greater purpose—to benefit the ummah. This was a good start, but it wasn't enough.

CHAPTER 15

By the next day, everyone was working. Brian was updating our social media pages and advertising the bake sale. Sam was putting up a sign-up sheet for people to bring in donations. Mike made us flyers, which we hung up around the masjid. I focused on planning an Islamic Quiz competition for next Friday's meeting, where younger kids would participate to win a prize. I decided the prize would be a $25 Amazon gift card, funded by the donations SALAAM had received. I also put together a small halaqah (Islamic lecture) on the five pillars of faith: Shahadah, Salah, Zakat, Sawm, and Hajj— the five things an individual must do to be considered a Muslim.

Before we knew it, Friday had arrived. I raced home after school, got changed, and then ran to the masjid. Everyone was moving quickly and setting up. I set the microphone for the competition, which would be starting shortly. Before the competition, I gave the halaqah. I didn't do much talking, as the younger kids insisted on explaining the five pillars themselves. Everyone found it really cute, and I took the opportunity to step into the lobby. There, I found Brian and Ali setting up for the bake sale. Some of the items were bought, and others were donated. An older woman walked up to me and handed me a tray.

"I baked brownies," she said, with a thick Hindi accent.

"Thank you so much," Ali replied. She handed the tray to him, and he set it on the table. Someone else had brought croissants. Aaliyah brought in chocolate chip cookies. Another girl from my school brought cupcakes, and a guy brought chips. Once everything was set up, the table looked incredibly full.

"I hope all of this is enough," Ali remarked.

"It will be," I replied.

"I've been meaning to ask you how you're doing. You've been through a lot, and things are happening so fast. It must be overwhelming."

"Well, I'm not gonna lie to you and say that I'm totally okay. Some days I am, and others I'm not. But I'm just taking it a step at a time, hoping it all works out. Sometimes I wonder what I was thinking when starting all of this. I'm just making myself a target again."

"But all of this is amazing. Don't you realize what

you're doing? You're building a community, Muhammad —one so strong that nothing will be able to break us."

"Thanks, but it's not just me. It's all of us. We're all building something together. I don't know what it is yet, but it's going to be amazing."

"Well, it's not going to build itself. Let's get back to work."

"Yes, let's do it."

The bake sale turned out to be a huge success, but it still wasn't enough to fund the carnival. That night, after the competition, I made an announcement to the crowd and explained our dilemma, hoping someone might have an idea. Although no one did, the donation box was full by the end of the meeting. Sam counted the money and said we now had just enough for the carnival. With Eid only two weeks away, we had to figure out how to get the carnival set up in time.

I sent a text in the SALAAM staff group chat, and Sheikh Omar replied that he knew of a company that had set up a carnival for the masjid a couple of years ago. He would contact them again to set up in the masjid's courtyard. Our job was to gather the food and find volunteers for the carnival. Ali texted a list of potential volunteers, which included him, me, Sam, Nouria, Walid (her older sister and brother), Mike, Amber, and Shawn (Sam's parents).

The next day at school, Ali, Sam, and I went to the

library together during lunch to come up with a plan. Our parents and Ali's siblings had agreed to volunteer, but even with our help, we still needed two more people.

"We're selling a lot of stuff, so we're going to need the extra help."

"How about your parents, Ali? Would they be willing to help?" Sam asked.

"Yeah, could you ask them?" I added.

Ali went quiet, his expression faltering as if on the verge of tears. He began fidgeting with the sleeves of his sweater, biting his bottom lip. Without saying anything, he stood up and slowly began to leave, but Sam stopped him.

"Are you okay? Was it something I said?" Sam asked.

"No, no, you're good. It's just that..." Ali hesitated.

"You don't have to say anything if you don't want to. We got you, man," I said.

"Yeah," Sam added, "I know we didn't start off very well. I get it if you don't wanna talk."

"Oh, no, it's fine. I know I can trust you guys. It's just that my parents died a couple of years ago. It's just me, Nouria, and Walid now. They're basically my parents. Walid dropped out of college to start working and make a living for us. He's my legal guardian now. Despite all they've done, all they've sacrificed for me, losing our parents still hurts. Even after all these years, the pain hasn't lessened. It's just that it feels wrong to say, you know? Like I shouldn't be saying this to you because I know your situation is a lot worse than mine, Muhammad. I mean, at least I have them. You have no one."

That stung a little, being reminded of that sad, but true fact so bluntly. Yes, I had people, but no blood relatives I knew of. I still wasn't about to show my disdain.

"Yeah, but that doesn't mean it hurts any less. And for the record, I don't have no one. I have you guys. Dude, we got each other. Allah puts people in your path for a reason, right?"

There was a heavy silence in the air. No one was sure what to say next. Sometimes, after such heavy words have been uttered, it's hard to know how to respond.

"Anyways, let's get back to work," Ali said suddenly, visibly wanting to change the subject. "Who else would be willing to volunteer? I mean, we already have Brian, but we could still use one more person. Oh wait! There's this guy in my English class, Samir. He's heard about all you do, and he told me he was willing to help if you needed him."

"Great! Is he Muslim? Not that it matters."

"I think so. He's Moroccan, so he probably is."

"Let's have an executive member-only meeting before that, so we can get to know him first."

"Okay, great. I'll let him know. Oh, and Sam, I just wanted to say I'm sorry again for what happened at the masjid. I mean, yeah, what you said was wrong, but I could have reacted differently."

"It's fine. I kinda deserved it. So we're good now, right?"

"Yeah, of course. We're chill."

At that moment, the bell rang, and we rushed to our separate classes. I couldn't stop thinking about Ali all day. Who knew that Ali, with his friendly demeanor, outgoing personality, and great ideas, had been through so much? It served as a reminder that everyone has their share of struggles. It felt nice to have someone to empathize with.

The next day was the SALAAM executive members' meeting. We usually have our meetings during lunch and then fill Brian in on what he missed. I headed to the library, where I found Ali and Sam, along with Samir. He was tall, visibly Arab, with light brown hair and matching big brown eyes. His voice was deep, and he had a full-grown beard, a sunnah of our beloved Prophet.

"Hey, what's up? I'm Samir. You're Muhammad, right?" he asked cheerfully, speaking with an accent. I guessed he had just recently learned English.

"Yup! Welcome aboard!" I replied.

"Thanks, it's so great to be working with you, bro. You're sensational at this point. So, you need me to help with the carnival, right?"

"I really appreciate the compliment, but trust me, I'm not all that. And yeah, we need more people to help out."

"Well, I'm down to help. So, what can I do?"

"Well, we need someone to walk around the carnival and make sure everything's working as it should. We also need you to promote SALAAM and the goals of the organization. If anyone needs help, has questions, or wants to give a donation, either assist them or direct them to me if you don't know how to. We don't need people for rides and entertainment since the company is covering that."

"Alright, sounds good. So, we're doing it on Eid morning, right after salah?"

"Yup, just come to the masjid a little earlier so we can go over things one final time."

"Okay, sure."

"God, I can't believe Eid is almost here," remarked Ali. "It feels like Ramadan just started."

"I know, right?" I replied. "I'm excited for Eid, but I wish Ramadan didn't have to end so fast. I just love the vibes and the imaan boost this month gives. I feel so much more connected—to Islam, to Allah, to everyone, really. Post-Ramadan blues are gonna hit hard for sure."

"Speaking of which, this Friday is the 27th night of Ramadan, the night most likely to be Laylatul Qadr. We should be expecting a lot of people at the masjid, so we should do something special."

"Yeah, I was thinking about the same thing the other day, but what should we do?"

"Maybe we should host a Quran competition, but make it bigger—like with judges and a bigger prize. We could also make it an annual event for every Ramadan, if we plan on continuing regular meetings."

"Good idea, but who will be the judges? I mean, I could be one since I'm a hafiz, but who else?"

"I only have forty chapters down, the longest being seventy-eight Ayahs. So, I doubt I'll be much help."

"Well," said Samir, "before I moved here, I was pretty close to completing hifz. I went to school in Morocco, and Islamic studies was embedded in our curriculum. I only have Surah Baqarah left, and I plan on tackling that soon, InshaAllah. I can help judge the competition if needed."

"Perfect!" I exclaimed. "Ali, you can be in charge of the younger kids with smaller Surahs. Since they won't be old enough to compete, you could run a scaled-down version of the competition, which Samir and I will oversee. And if you can read Quranic Arabic, it'll be perfect since you won't have to memorize anything else."

"All right!" Ali replied. "We'll focus on the last part of the Quran, since that's the smallest. You and Samir can be the main judges. Sorry, we're excluding you, Sam."

"Oh no, it's fine," Samir said. "It's just that you guys are lucky to be so close to your faith—"

"When you start seeing your faith as a way of life, you just become indescribably close to it," I replied. "Islam for me is a way of life, one that I wouldn't give up for anything."

"Yeah, that must be nice. If it's okay, could I skip this meeting? I just feel uncomfortable, and I know I'd be out of place." He looked uneasy.

"What the heck? Of course you're not out of place. It's an interfaith event. The competition is the only part that's exclusive to Muslims. There will be other things, too, that we'll need your help with. Brian will be there as well—he's not Muslim."

"You said this was supposed to be interfaith. Interfaith means all faiths should be included in everything. Don't you think a Quran competition is too Muslim-dominated? I get that Islam means a lot to you, but it's not like that for everyone. The whole purpose of SALAAM was to make Islam known and have people respect it, but now it honestly feels like you're trying to convert them."

"I dunno, maybe you're right. We should definitely stay away from the Quran competition and not go into depth about Islam. We'll keep it focused on a genuine, raw interaction between different faiths. We'll just get rid of it."

"What! No, don't get rid of it. Just keep it separate and optional for those who want to stay after the meetings. That way, others won't feel obligated to sit through it. SALAAM can still live up to its goal."

"Alright, good point. We'll postpone the Quran competition until after the meeting so it'll be totally optional. That way, we'll be sharing Islam while getting Muslims closer to their faith, benefiting both communities. I'll text you guys if there are any updates."

And with that, the bell rang, and we all rushed to our

next classes. Things were falling into place beautifully, and I had Allah to thank for it. Alhamdulillah for everything. My success is by Him and Him alone. I quickly made a dua, praying that things would stay this way and continue to unfold according to plan.

CHAPTER 16

Before we knew it, the twenty-seventh night of Ramadan arrived. After this, there would only be a couple of days left until Eid. We had been meeting constantly, contacting the company, making arrangements for food, and keeping the masjid updated. We all went to school and met during lunch to finalize the details. The prize for the Quran competition this time would be a Quran with the winner's name engraved in it. To make it even more exciting, we'd have separate rounds, with competitors being eliminated based on their memorization, adherence to tajweed rules, and pronunciation.

The food would be provided by a nearby restaurant, and the topic of the day would be peace—the definition of *Salaam*. I figured it would get people to really think about the irony of how Islam revolves around the concept of peace, yet people still associate it with violence. It was messed up, and the world needed to see that. They needed to differentiate between Islam and people. Muslims aren't perfect, but Islam is.

When we got home, Brian and I quickly got ready and headed to the masjid. Mike said he'd meet us there after work. "You guys got this," he had said. Upon arrival, we saw that Ali, Nouria, and Walid had already arrived, and with them was Sam. They had picked up the food from the restaurant and set it up with the help of Sheikh Omar, who assured us that everything was ready for the Eid carnival on Monday. He also told us that we had all done a great job.

"The masjid community has never been this big before. You truly are incredible, Muhammad. All of you are."

I thanked him for all of his help. We quickly broke our fast, prayed maghrib, and got ready for the club meeting. At the meeting, I made a short speech, thanking everyone for being there and discussing the definition of *Salaam*.

"Peace is the center of Islam and, therefore, the core foundation of this organization."

Ali made some announcements regarding the Eid carnival, then we ate and discussed the topic of the day— kindness. Kindness needs no religion, and as cliché as it may sound, it really does make the world a better place. A greeting, an affectionate touch, a word of empathy—it could mean the world to someone. It takes more energy to hate than to love. A lot could have been avoided if people recognized that.

"None of you have believed unless you want for your brother what you want for yourself," a verse from the Quran that encourages all Muslims to think of their faith as one. Imaan expands far beyond the scope of one person—it's about the entire ummah.

We then talked about Ramadan and how the 27th night was especially important to Muslims. Soon, instead of just talking separately, everyone was engaged in a lively conversation about Ramadan. For some, this was their first exposure to the holy month, while for others, it was their first time having a community to celebrate and observe with. SALAAM had changed their lives for the better in that sense. I sat back, watching in awe of what we had created.

The meeting went well, and nobody seemed to want to leave. People lingered for hours, talking and laughing. The sense of community was amazing. Bonds were being formed—friendships that would hopefully last a lifetime. By the time Mike arrived, we had just started the Quran competition. Ali took the younger kids to another room where they would have their own version, while I led the older ones to the prayer room, where a microphone was set up. Parents and even some non-Muslim SALAAM club members sat in the audience, where we had set up chairs earlier.

Samir and I sat up front and called the names of each

child who auditioned. After several rounds, only two contestants remained: a young girl named Aisha and a boy named Ibrahim. We tested them both on various parts of some of the longest surahs of the Quran. We took notes on each recitation, then went into the Imam's office to discuss the winner in private. After a brief discussion, we both agreed on one winner.

I started to get up to announce the winner, but Samir stopped me.

"Wait, before we announce the winner, don't you think it would be nice to end the competition with us both reciting something?" he asked.

"What do you mean? Like reciting the Quran? I haven't recited anything in public since my hifz graduation. Since… you know, since before what happened. Bruh, I don't know about this."

"Well, you never will unless you try it, man. There's no better time than the present. If they could do it, so could we. Right?"

I could see that he had his mind set on this. Although I hadn't known him for long, from what Ali had told me, he was very determined.

"Alright, fine, but you have to go first."

"Deal."

"Salaam, everyone!" Samir began. "First off, we'd like to congratulate everyone on a job well done. All of the recitations were spectacular, and we had a hard time choosing the winner. May Allah reward all of you for your efforts, and please continue building your bond with His book, even after this competition. Before we announce the winner, Muhammad and I would like to wrap up this evening with our own recitations. I'll start, and Muhammad will follow."

He then began reciting Surah Yaseen, the verses flowing off his tongue. The room fell silent as his voice grew stronger, his pronunciation clear, emphasizing the verses about Allah's forgiveness and the reward awaiting believers in Jannah. When he reached the halfway point, he stopped and nodded at me. Without saying a word, I took the microphone and picked up right where he left off.

At first, I started slowly, nervous about being in front of a crowd again. But then I closed my eyes, pictured myself alone, and my voice grew louder. The stuttering stopped, and my recitation became smoother. I immersed myself in the meanings of the verses, picturing myself at my hifz graduation, on stage with my parents beaming at me, and my friends and family cheering me on. I allowed that image to consume me, almost as if I could make it real. If I imagined it enough, maybe it would become true. I could wake up from the nightmare that had been my life for the past year—the accident, the move, the shooting, Mr. Carter, the video. It would all fade, and I'd find myself at my hifz graduation, with none of it ever having happened.

But then I realized—SALAAM wouldn't have existed.

Mike and Brian wouldn't be in my life. Ali, Sam, Samir, and all of my friends and teachers from Willow Heights wouldn't be part of my life. I thought back to when I had opened the Quran out of desperation and recited Surah Yaseen, lost, scared, and confused. I still felt that way, but I had come a long way since then. The Quran had served as a guide. Allah had served as a guide. He found me lost and guided me, just as He did for Prophet Muhammad in Surah Duha. I had been far from Him, but all it took was one step to return. I walked toward Him, and He ran to me.

I opened my eyes and realized I had finished reciting without even realizing it. I looked around, taking in everything that had happened and the new life I was fortunate to have. I noticed that everyone else had tears in their eyes. All the SALAAM members stared at me in awe and emotion. I got off stage and walked over to my family—not a foster family, not an adopted family, just my family. I realized that accepting Mike and Brian as my family didn't mean I had to let go of Mom, Dad, and Maryam. They were a part of me and would live on inside me. Their memory would never be erased, even as I allowed new people into my life. It was Mike and Brian who had helped me see that.

I went over to Brian. He looked at me and said, "Muhammad, that was... wow." I smiled. Mike looked at me, his face full of wonder. "How did you do that, Muhammad? That was incredible. It was just indescribably passionate, melodic, beautiful... I'm at a loss for words!"

Just then, the room erupted into applause. Everyone rose and applauded. Samir stepped on stage. "Thank you, everyone. Now, without further ado, we will announce the winner of our first annual Ramadan Quran Competition."

Right. The competition. I had almost forgotten about it. I walked onto the stage and took the microphone. "Congratulations to Ibrahim Ali! Please come up to the stage to receive your prize and a certificate of recognition!"

The room broke out into applause once more as Ibrahim beamed with pride. I smiled and handed him his certificate. He reminded me so much of myself when I was younger—the same attachment to and love for the Quran that had driven me to dedicate years to memorizing and understanding it. I handed him the card he could exchange for a Quran, one that Sheikh Omar would engrave his name in. I leaned in and whispered in his ear, "You did amazing! Don't stop here. Go for hifz. You can memorize the whole book if you set your mind to it. If I can do it, so can you."

He smiled. "That's what I'm working towards, inshallah."

"Inshallah," I replied.

He asked to take a photo with me and the SALAAM crew, and we of course agreed. Soon, more people came up to ask for photos. As I stood there, I realized that not only had I helped non-Muslims start to respect Islam more, but I had also helped Muslims become closer to their faith. I was steps closer to serving the ummah, closer to fulfilling a much greater purpose—the purpose I had anticipated at the start of SALAAM.

CHAPTER 17

We hung out for the rest of the night, chatting with the guests and congratulating the participants. After a lot of photos, selfies, prayers, celebrations, and cleaning up, it was finally time to go home. I said goodbye to Ali and his family, then to Sam and Samir as they left, and finally joined my family as we headed off together.

When we got home, we were all exhausted, so we went straight to bed. The next morning, Brian came into my room. We were going to work on editing this week's video for the SALAAM YouTube channel, but we were really behind since I had no idea what to do. Then Brian showed me some of the videos he had recorded the night before, including Samir's and my joint recitation of Surah Yaseen.

"Why don't we post this?" he asked. "We can add the definition of each verse at the bottom."

"I don't know," I replied. "We'll have to check with Samir to make sure she's okay with it."

"It's worth a try. Text him. You both sound amazing, and this will definitely help the views go up."

"Okay, I guess. I mean, it's worth a try."

So, I sent Samir a text and waited for his reply. While I waited, Brian and I got to work editing the video. We added subtitles with the English translation of each line, then inserted a transition between Samir's part and mine. We got everything set up, leaving just the upload. Just then, Samir's text came through. He said he was fine with the video going up. At that, Brian clicked upload, and we waited.

The video got a lot of views—almost as many as the first one we posted. It also received numerous comments asking for more Quranic recitations. I spoke with Samira, and she agreed that we should definitely do more together, and even that I should try some solo recitations. I asked Brian and the others for their opinions, and they all agreed. SALAAM was growing, but it was also very random—like a bunch of puzzle pieces we were still trying to figure out how to piece together. The end result was still unclear, but we were making progress.

I spent all of Sunday at the masjid, helping get everything set up for the carnival the next day. I helped clear the courtyard where the company would set up early in the morning, then brought up some tables for the food. I carried picnic tables to the parking lot, set chairs aside with my friends, and even laid out the carpets for prayer. Afterward, I broke my last fast, Ali led us in dua, and I read some Quran.

"It's really over, guys," I finally said.

"Yeah, but we have next year, InshaAllah," Samir said, interrupting. "And we have so much to look forward to even now."

"I literally cannot wait for tomorrow!" Ali added, biting into a cookie. "Eid hits differently every year."

I couldn't say anything to that.

At home, I checked the YouTube channel and saw that the views had gone up significantly. I realized we needed to post more often, so I asked Brian to vlog everything that happened at the masjid the next day.

Monday morning, we woke up, got dressed, and headed straight to the masjid. There, we met Sheikh Omar, Ali, and his family.

"Eid Mubarak, guys!" I called out.

"Heyyy, Eid Mubarak!" Sheikh Omar responded. "Let's get to work, everyone."

I looked around—the company had already set everything up, and we spent the next half hour setting up the food. Once everything was set up, we went inside, where everyone had already arrived for the Eid Salah. I sat down, listening to Sheikh Omar give the Eid Takbeer and Khutbah. Then everyone stood for the actual prayer.

Once we were done, I immediately ran outside to get to work.

At that point, people started arriving for the carnival—many from SALAAM and others who had heard about it. Passersby stopped to check things out, and we invited them to join in. I caught up to Ali, Samir, Sam, and Brian and made sure they knew what their tasks were. Nouria, Walid, and Sam's parents also started helping out. Mike began handing out goody bags to kids, and I focused on making sure all the games were running smoothly. We spent the morning like this, with no set end time for the carnival, but people began leaving around noon to continue with their other Eid plans. Soon, we were the only ones left. All the volunteers regrouped to help clean up, and the company began packing up and leaving. Sheikh Omar handed out garbage bags, and we all pitched in. Some bystanders saw us cleaning and joined in.

The Rabbi from a nearby synagogue approached me and congratulated me on a job well done. He said the carnival was a great idea and allowed people of different faiths to come together over something greater than religion. He told me he would love to collaborate with us again on future events and help tackle the stigma surrounding both of our religions. I took that to mean we had accomplished our goal.

Once we finished, everyone else started heading

home, leaving just me, Brian, Aaliyah, Sam, and Samir. The five of us hung around outside the masjid.

"Why don't we go inside?" Samir asked.

"S-sure," I responded. I led the way inside, but as soon as I entered, I started hyperventilating. Everywhere I looked, I saw the residue of the shooting. Suddenly, I started gasping for air. Samir put his arm around me.

"It's okay, Muhammad," he smiled. "We can wait outside."

And so, we did just that.

"We did it!" Ali exclaimed. "We really did it! Bro, this was so cool. Alhumdulilah."

"Yup, Alhumdulilah. It was a very successful morning. Well, an entire month, really," Samir agreed. "But what are we going to do now? I mean, it is Eid. We should probably get going to our respective families."

"Yeah, I have to go home soon," Ali said. "Nouria, Walid, and I are driving up to Albany to visit our aunt and uncle. We do that every year."

He had a tradition to follow. Even after losing his parents, he still had something to remember this day by. I couldn't help but feel a little jealous.

"Nice, what do you do there?" I asked.

"Well, we mostly just hang out with our cousins in the area. Sometimes, we all spend the night and gather for breakfast the next morning. It's really fun."

"I should probably get home too," Sam suddenly said. "My family doesn't celebrate, but I have a lot of homework to catch up on. So, I'll see you guys later." And with that, he left.

"My mom just texted me," Samir said. "I totally forgot my cousins were coming over for Eid, so I have to go home now."

"Well," I began, "you go on and have fun, and we'll see you tomorrow, InshaAllah. Eid Mubarak!"

"Are you going to be okay?" Ali asked. "I know this is your first Eid without your family."

"Yeah," Samir replied. "Do you want to come over? My mom said I could invite friends."

"Thanks, guys, but I think I'll be okay. Go celebrate with your families. Eid Mubarak!" I said, trying to muster up the most convincing smile I could.

"Eid Mubarak!" They both said at once before running off.

Brian and I headed home. I was silent most of the way, soaking in the rush of the city around us. It was funny how, despite the way my heart sank, the world kept on moving. This was one of the most important and, at the same time, hardest days for me. For everyone else, it was just another day.

I was excited for Eid and how I would be spending it this year. I threw myself into SALAAM and the carnival plans, trying to fill the hole left by my family, but no matter what I did, it still hurt that it wouldn't be the same as previous years. As much as I loved my new family and embraced my new life, a part of me was still wishing for my old one.

Today was making the void inside my heart, which I had started to close, open once again. The pain was excruciating. It hurt to know that it would never be the same again. It hurt to know I would never look at this day the same way again. A day once full of joy and happiness would now be full of remembrance.

"Are you sure you're going to be okay?" Brian asked, suddenly breaking the silence. "I get that this must be really hard for you, especially since we don't celebrate in my family."

I just nodded and tried to avert his gaze. When we got home, I immediately headed for my room. I couldn't get over what Brian had said about not celebrating Eid in *his* family. For so long, I had thought of Mike and Brian as my family, and although I knew he had said it subconsciously and didn't mean anything by it, it hurt when Brian said "my family" instead of "our family." It was like he was separating me from them, like I didn't fully belong.

The truth was, I may never fully belong. I belonged with Mom, Dad, and Maryam. And now they were gone.

I took out Maryam's journal and opened it to an entry she had written last year. It was a poem about Ramadan:

How we have awaited you
Oh blessed month of Ramadan,
How we have missed awakening,
Praying, eating, and rejoicing,
Until the next dawn.
How we have awaited you,
Waiting for you to strengthen our imaan.
How we have missed completing khatams,
Spending long mornings reading the Quran.
How we have missed racing to the masjid to pray taraweeh,
Friends and families gathering in rows,
Reciting Quran in unison and ending with Ameen.
How we have missed gathering together
To break our fasts,
With a large iftar,
Then gathering to pray Maghrib and make istighfar.
How we have missed giving our zakah to those in need,
Helping each other,
Improving ourselves and doing good deeds.
How we have missed qiyamulail,
Spending the entire night in ibadah.
We repent, spill our struggles to Allah, and ask Him to avail.
How we have missed suhoor,
Waking up before the sun for the pre-dawn meal,
Preparing for the day of fasting, just as we had the day before.
How we have missed those last ten nights,
Worshiping Allah intently,
Trying to make our wrongs right.

Ramadan, month of Islam,
Ramadan, month of imaan,
Ramadan, month of the Quran.

I thought of last Eid. We had spent the morning at the masjid, volunteering and serving breakfast to the community. Once the crowd cleared, we headed home, where all our friends gathered since it was our turn to host the annual Eid party. Maryam, Mom, and I spent the night before cooking, while Mom and Maryam decorated their arms with henna and picked out their abayas for the next day. Dad and I got our clothes ready and set up the Eid breakfast table. All that was left to do in the morning was make the tea.

We always drank tea and ate cookies on Eid morning. It kept us going through the Eid prayer, and afterward, we would have another breakfast at the masjid. Everyone would bring something, and my mom always made Mseman, a traditional Moroccan bread. Everyone loved it, and it would be gone in minutes.

I laughed as I remembered how my parents would bump into each other in the kitchen while making the Eid tea. They would smile, and Mom would playfully slap Dad on the back. "What did I get myself into marrying this one?" she would laugh. "You were too in love to think straight," Dad would retort, kissing her on the forehead.

My mom always made Moroccan mint tea, and Dad made chai. I always drank the mint tea, while Maryam only drank chai. Despite being half Moroccan and half Pakistani, I always felt more connected to my Moroccan side. I spoke fluent Arabic but only minimal Urdu because my mom spoke only Arabic to Maryam and me, while Dad spoke only English to us. My parents had a strange mix of English and Arabic when they spoke to each other. Dad knew a little Arabic from a class he took in college. Our house was a blend of different cultures—Arab, South Asian, and American. I loved it, and at that moment, I would have given anything to go back to it. To relive its familiarity. One more time. Just once again.

I was so lost in thought that I didn't hear the knocking on my door. Mike opened it. "Are you alright, Muhammad?" he asked. I nodded and tried to turn away, but I felt a lump in my throat.

"Do you want to talk?"

I got up and tried to leave, but he blocked the doorway. I sat back down.

"Hey, look. Trust me, I know this is hard. I can't pretend to know just how hard it is, and that would be unfair. You've gone through the unimaginable, and only you know how tough it really is. But you're still standing, and that's amazing. There will be highs and lows. I'll be here through all of them, I promise."

He paused, then continued. "I know how important this day is to you. And I also know that no matter how hard we try, we can't make this day what it used to be. But we're here for you. Whatever you need. You'll never lose us. I can't replace your parents—and we won't try—but I'll always be here. You may have lost them, but I am here for the long haul."

I got up and hugged him. I tried to swallow the growing lump in my throat, but it was pointless. I dissolved into tears.

"I'm sorry," I blurted out. "I'm really sorry."

I didn't know what I was apologizing for, but it felt right. At that moment, I was shaking, and Mike just held me. He didn't say anything, and he didn't need to. It just felt good to have him there with me. I needed someone there. I didn't realize it, but I did.

At that moment, Brian walked in, but Mike told him to give me a minute. He left without saying a word. I was grateful. I didn't want him to see me like this. I knew from the last time he saw me crying at the library that he wouldn't make fun of me or think less of me, but it was still awkward—especially over something like this.

"What did you usually do on Eid?" Mike asked at last. "I mean, besides going to the masjid. What did you do with your family?"

I told him about how the night before Eid would go and about breakfast the next day. I also told him about the party we would have afterward, how Mom, Maryam, and I would spend so much time cooking. I shared how everyone would stay late into the night, talking, laughing, eating, and having fun. On the second day of Eid, they would come back again to help clean up, and we would end up talking, laughing, and eating all over again.

Talking about it was hard. I knew I was talking about something that would never happen again, but it was also nice to share my old life. I would never truly move forward if I didn't learn how to look back on the past from time to time.

"That sounds like fun," Mike replied. "I think it's too late to have a party that big, but come out to the kitchen. Maybe we can make some of that tea."

CHAPTER 18

I dragged my feet into the kitchen, not wanting to be there but also not wanting to disappoint Mike when, all of a sudden, there was a knock on the door. Brian came out of his room and asked me to open it. Confused about what was going on, I obeyed, and there stood Sam and his parents, carrying trays of food.

"Sam? Dude, what are you doing here?" I asked, perplexed.

"Eid Mubarak!" he exclaimed with a hilarious accent. "I know we can't bring your old Eid traditions back, but we can make new ones together."

His mom handed me the trays. "These are for you guys."

"Thank you so much!" I replied. "Please, come on in!"

And so they entered, and I went back into the kitchen

to finish making the tea. I took out teacups and saucers and arranged the contents on a tray. Then Brian brought out the trays of food, and we went back to the living room to hear the Eid Takbeer playing on the TV.

"Allahu Akbar, Allahu Akbar, Allahu Akbar, Lailillah illa Allah. Allahu Akbar, Allahu Akbar, Walilahi lhamd."

It sounded familiar. It sounded like home. Like Eid the way I remembered it. Ever since I was little, I would wake up to the Eid Takbeer every morning on this day. I smiled and set the tea down on the table.

I went back into the kitchen and opened a tray of chocolate chip cookies and cake that Sam had also brought. I set everything out on plates and brought it to the living room. Just as I sat down to hang out with Sam and Brian, there was another knock on the door. Brian got up and opened it, and there were Ali, Nouria, and Walid. I was baffled.

"What are you guys doing here?" I asked. "Aren't you supposed to be in Albany?"

"Surprise!" exclaimed Ali. "You really thought we were gonna leave you alone on Eid? I only used that as an excuse to go home and get everything ready! Brian, Sam, and I have been planning this for a while. We want your first Eid in New York to be special. We got you, bro!"

"This is for you," said Walid, setting down a bag on the table. "We should probably get going now," he added, glancing at Nouria.

"What? No! Please stay, it's Eid!" I blurted.

He smiled and then sat down. I opened the bag and found a container of cookies and a small package.

"That's an Eid gift for you," said Ali. "Open it."

"What? Why? Bro, come on, you didn't have to do that. You guys being here is more than enough."

"Ya Allah! Just open it already. I've been dying to see your reaction."

I ripped open the package, and inside was a silver chain. On it was God's name, *Allah*, written in Arabic calligraphy. Ali smiled at me and said, "This is to remind you that all of the obstacles that life threw at you were a test from Him. And none of the good things that have happened to you would have happened without Him. He is closer to you than your jugular vein, so now you can keep His name close to it. Sorry, I'm rambling."

I put it on and smiled. "Thank you," I said. "Seriously, thank you, all of you. This is incredible. JazakAllah Khair."

For the next couple of hours, we all just talked, laughed, and ate. It felt amazing to be surrounded by people who cared enough to go out of their way to do something special for me. Around six in the evening, there was another knock on the door. I opened it, and there stood Samir with a woman who I guessed was his mom.

"Samir? What are you doing here? Did you guys all plan to come together?"

"The three of us did," said Ali, gesturing over to Brian and Sam, "but we had no idea he would be here as well."

"Well, I didn't plan on it," said Samir. "But when I told my mom about you, she said that we had to come over. So, Eid Mubarak!"

"Eid Mubarak!" exclaimed his mom. "So you're Muhammad, right?" she asked in Arabic.

"Yes, Ma'am, that's me," I responded in Arabic.

"I've heard so much about you! You can call me Auntie Jameela. When Samir told me about you, we had to stop by. This is such a special day, and we can't imagine how hard it must be for you to spend it without your family for the first time. I made Msemen," she said with a smile, handing me a bag.

"That's so kind of you. Thank you so much! Please, join us."

They came inside, and we all sat down again and started talking. Brian, Sam, Ali, Samir, and I drifted off to my bedroom while our parents stayed in the living room. We started talking, first about SALAAM and the events of the carnival earlier that day. Then, eventually, we started talking about school and complaining about all the homework, regents prep, and AP stress we had to look forward to after Eid. Before we knew it, two hours had gone by, and it was time for Sam, Ali, Samir, and their families to head home. I said goodbye and thanked them for everything. They didn't know how much I had needed them.

I closed the door behind them and came back inside, smiling.

"So, how was your Eid now?" asked Mike while pouring himself another cup of tea.

"Amazing, thank you so much," I replied. I turned to Brian. "Thanks for planning this," I said, touching the chain that Ali gave me. "You have no idea how much I needed it. Eid is special again." I looked up at the ceiling with a smile. "Thank you, Maryam. Thank you, Mama and Baba. Thank you, Allah."

That night, I opened the journal Brian had given me and made another entry:

"Dear Maryam,
I never thought I'd ever be able to enjoy Eid again, I wrote, but I was wrong. Once again, my new family proved me wrong."

I sighed contentedly, read a few entries from Maryam's journal, and then drifted off to sleep.

The next morning, as I was about to leave for school, I suddenly remembered that I wasn't fasting. I sat down and ate breakfast. I had forgotten what it felt like to eat during the day. It was nice, but also a little weird, like I was doing something wrong. My body was still in Ramadan mode, and every Muslim joked about how surreal the day after Eid felt in that way.

I met up with Brian and my friends on the subway,

and once we got to school, we headed to our separate classes. When I walked into my first-period history class, I was met with a surprise—Mr. Davis was back.

"Did you guys miss me?" he asked, laughing. Everyone cheered, and I never thought I'd be so happy to see him. After everything with Mr. Carter, we had been getting substitute after substitute, and it had been a mess. None of them knew what to teach us, and with the Global History Regents and AP World exams approaching in May, we were studying like crazy just to finish on time. In that one period, we had gone through three lessons.

I knew I'd be fine for the Regents, even though it was my first one, but the AP exam intimidated me. I'd taken APs last year and did well, but with how chaotic my life had been, I wasn't so sure anymore. By the time class ended, I was exhausted. I dragged myself to my next class —Algebra 2. It turned out we had a Regents review in that class too.

I sighed and took out my notebook. I started copying notes and answering questions. I was good at math and was hoping to skip Precalc next year and jump straight into Calc BC. Halfway through class, I got a text from Sam. (Ms. Miller didn't mind us checking our phones occasionally as long as we got back to work.)

I took out my phone and read his text. He asked if I wanted to hang out in Central Park after school—just us and Brian. I agreed and sent a quick reply. Then, I tucked my phone away and returned to work. My brain was fried after answering forty questions in one period. I looked forward to hanging out; Eid had been fun, and I loved how much closer I was getting to my friends.

Later that day, the three of us got on the subway and headed for Central Park. When we arrived, we sat at a table and worked on our homework together. Just as we were finishing, I got a call from Mike.

"Hey, Muhammad. I know we said you could hang out with your friends this afternoon, but could you come home now? We need to talk to you about something," he said, sounding slightly concerned.

"Is everything okay?" I asked.

"Yes, love, everything's fine. We just need you home right now."

"Alright, Brian and I are coming." I told everyone about the call, and we decided to head home.

Brian and I walked to the subway station. "Your dad seemed worried on the phone. I don't know what's going on. I hope it's nothing bad."

"It'll be alright. He exaggerates sometimes."

"I hope you're right."

When we arrived, Mike greeted us with a smile. "Hey! How was your day?"

"Good. Is everything okay?"

"Oh, yes. Everything's fine. Did I worry you guys? Oh my god, I'm so sorry. I just needed to talk to Muhammad about something. Brian, can you go to your room?"

"No, he can stay. Whatever it is, I don't mind."

"Alright then. Muhammad, I want you to know that you don't have to do this if you don't want to, and if you decide to, I'll be there for you every step of the way."

"Don't want to do what?"

"Well, we got a letter from court asking for you to show up as a victim of the shooting at the masjid. You're going to stand in front of the judge and jury and tell them what happened. At the end, you can face the attackers and confront them one on one if you want to. The only thing required by the court is for you to share your account of what happened."

I glanced at the arm the bullet had grazed. The doctor had said it had healed completely, leaving only a large scar that would fade with time. My injuries had healed—the bruises and cuts were gone. But I still hadn't healed internally.

The shooting had happened at the worst time possible. I was still haunted by nightmares and trying to overcome the trauma of losing my family when, suddenly, I had even more to endure. The nightmares grew more frequent. I would wake up, unable to fall back asleep. Entering the masjid alone still made me anxious. I always made sure someone was with me—someone to turn to, just in case. Even praying there wasn't the same anymore. May Allah forgive me, but I would feel anxious in sujood, waiting for the prayer to end, longing to go home.

I tried to block everything out, channeling all my

energy into SALAAM, school, and my friends. But my past always found its way back, crawling out from that little corner in my mind I desperately tried to lock away. Thinking about it made me shudder. I touched my Allah pendant and looked up at Mike. "When do we have to be there?"

"Next week. The trial starts, but it will probably last at least a month. Are you sure you're ready?"

"I'll never fully be ready, but I have to do this."

"Alright then. I'm proud of you, you know? Let's eat dinner, and we can talk more if you want to."

That night, I had another nightmare. I walked into the masjid, and faceless men with guns were shooting people down. I saw Maryam, lifeless on the ground, her beautiful face covered in blood. On the other side, Brian, Mike, Samir, Ali, and Ahmad were calling for me to run. They were running toward me, but their steps were slow, like time had slowed, and no matter how hard they tried, they couldn't reach me. It felt like minutes passed, frozen in time.

Then I saw him. The man who fired the bullet that grazed my arm. His face had always been a blur in my memory, but now, in my dream, it was crystal clear. He smirked cruelly, a look of triumph in his eyes, as if he'd been waiting for this moment. He pointed his gun at me.

"No!" I screamed. "No, not again! No!" I raised my arms to shield my face, but it was too late. BOOM! He fired, and once again, everything went black.

I woke up shivering, the fear from the dream still gripping me. I went to the kitchen, grabbed a glass of water, and pulled my Quran from the shelf. I sat back down on my bed, opened it to a random page, and started reading. I kept reading until I unknowingly drifted to sleep, only to be jolted awake by my alarm for school. I hugged the Quran tightly, holding it close to my chest for ten minutes, reciting a few prayers of protection over and over. Then I got ready, and Brian and I left.

On the subway, I stood as close to Brian as possible, keeping my head down, focused on the floor. A man across from me reached into his pocket, and for a moment, I thought he was pulling out a gun. My heart raced until the train finally arrived at our stop, and I practically ran out of the station.

"Muhammad, you good? You seemed anxious on the train."

"Yeah, I'm fine. The subway just makes me nervous sometimes."

"Why didn't you tell me earlier? We could take the bus to school. I didn't know the subway scared you that much. I guess we're usually so busy talking about SALAAM, I didn't notice."

"Yeah, it's fine." But the truth was, it wasn't fine. The bus wouldn't make it better. Anywhere with unfamiliar people felt scary. Closing the door on that reality was getting harder and harder. I sighed and went to class.

Spanish was first period. I sat at my desk and started

my work without saying a word. Mr. Martinez's voice felt distant, and all I could think about was facing the shooters in court. It was something I had always known was coming, but I thought it would be in the far-off future. By then, I imagined I would be a smarter, braver Muhammad—someone who knew how to compose himself and say the right things. I never realized how unrealistic that was.

It was scary, even being in the now familiar school, surrounded by people I was beginning to trust. I wasn't sure who I could rely on anymore. I didn't know who genuinely cared and who might want to hurt me. I wasn't ready. How could I be ready to confront the people who caused me so much pain if I couldn't even face the pain itself?

For months, I had tried to push the horrifying memories of the attack out of my head by focusing on my new life. But I couldn't move on until I faced my past—and that meant confronting my emotions. I thought of the day Brian gave me the journal. Until then, I had been doing the same thing with The Accident, pushing it away and causing myself more pain. It wasn't until I accepted the journal, started writing, and broke down in front of Mike on Eid that I began to heal. I was going to do the same thing now. No more hiding. I would walk into the courtroom and say what I needed to say. I had no reason to hide or be afraid. I wasn't the one who did anything wrong. But before that, I had to confront my emotions.

I was going to feel safe again, but I knew I would need help to get there. So, I went up to Mr. Martinez and asked if I could talk to him after class. He had helped me with Mr. Carter and SALAAM, and I trusted that he would help me now.

I waited until the bell rang, then approached his desk.

"What's up, Muhammad?" he asked, smiling. "You were quiet all period. Do you need help with the lesson?"

"No, actually, I need help with something else. It's... well, it's a lot of things, and I'm not sure how to phrase it or what to ask for. This past year has been the hardest of my life. As you know, I lost my parents, and then the shooting happened. Looking back, I realize I've been pushing my feelings away, trying to focus on other things. But now I've just found out I have to go to court to face the attackers, and I don't know how to feel about that. All those emotions are rushing back, and I'm scared. Really scared. The people I trusted most are gone, and I don't know who to turn to anymore."

Mr. Martinez listened quietly, then spoke softly, "Well," he began, "first of all, I want you to know that you can trust me. You can talk to me about anything. And I'm sure Mike would be there for you too. There are people who care about you, and you don't have to go through this alone. Don't forget that."

"Thank you," I said, unsure of what else to say.

"Now, usually, I'd suggest the school counseling services, but given everything you've been through, I think therapy might be a better option. I know a really good therapist, Dr. Myers. He specializes in childhood trauma. Here's his card. Talk it over with your family and give him a call, okay?"

I took the card, thanked him, and left. He was right. I needed help.

CHAPTER 19

A few days later, I found myself in a whimsical waiting room, covered in colorful posters and shelves stocked with books and games. It reminded me of the waiting room at the pediatrician's office Maryam and I used to go to when we were younger. It didn't give off any therapy vibes. Mike signed us in, and we sat down on the bright red chairs. After about fifteen minutes, the receptionist called us in. We walked down a hallway into a small office. The office was decorated similarly to the waiting room, with posters of young children and a table filled with toys and games. There was even a small corner with bean bag chairs.

Behind the desk sat a man who looked not much older than me. He had light brown hair and a carefree smile. The environment was welcoming, and surprisingly, I found myself wanting to stay. Just being in the room made some of my anxiety melt away. If this was what therapy was all about, I was in.

"I'm Dr. Meyers," said the man. "It's nice to meet you, Muhammad." He turned to Mike. "Since this is our first session, I'd like to talk to Muhammad one-on-one. Is that okay with both of you?"

He turned to me when he said the last part. It felt nice, like he was including me in the decision.

"Of course," Mike said. "I'll be right outside if you need me, Muhammad."

Once they left, instead of sitting behind his desk, Dr. Meyers pulled over a chair and sat next to me. "So, how old are you?"

"I'm fifteen, turning sixteen in a few days."

"Oh, so you're in high school. How's that going?"

"It's okay. I'm just trying to get by after everything."

"How have you been adjusting to the change?"

I didn't answer. I looked down and started fidgeting with my Allah pendant.

"We don't have to talk about it right away," he said quickly. "Our schedule isn't rigid; we can go with whatever you want. You can tell me whatever you want. And if you don't want to talk, we can just sit here and do nothing. You're safe here, and we'll do whatever makes you comfortable. What do you like to do for fun?"

"Besides SALAAM, I really like basketball."

"Basketball? Do you play? Like on a team?"

"I used to, before everything that happened."

"I used to play in high school. I played varsity my freshman year, was captain by sophomore year, and got a scholarship for college because of it."

"Wow. Really? That's so cool. I've always wanted to go all the way with basketball."

We spent the rest of the session talking about basketball and college. He even gave me some tips on the application process. Not once did he bring up the shooting or my family. I found it fun—so much so that I forgot I was in therapy. It felt like talking to Ahmad, or Brian, or Sam. Like talking to a friend.

When I left, I felt like the imaginary chain that had been holding me back had finally broken. I was so close to the door, and I felt happy—really happy, not pretending or hiding anything. I felt exposed, completely transparent, but in a good way. When I got home, I called Ahmad.

"You sound happier," he told me.

"Dude, you sound like the old Muhammad."

For the first time in a long time, I was beginning to feel like the old Muhammad. We spent an hour talking, and I told him about the court hearing.

"Bro, I wish I could be there. We all miss you."

"I'll try visiting, InshaAllah, soon."

The first day of the court hearing was the next day. I got ready and went to bed. But when I woke up, the clarity I'd felt the day before was gone. I was a nervous wreck—more so than I was for the TV interview. I showered, got dressed, and sat at the edge of my bed with my head in my hands.

Brian came in and found me like that.

"Are you ready?" he asked.

"Ready as I'll ever be," I sighed. "I can do this." I was trying to convince myself more than I was trying to convince him.

I got up, and together we headed out. Mike met us outside, and we left.

In front of the courthouse, I felt an unexpected calmness. Whatever happens, happens. There's nothing I can do about it. It's all in Allah's hands, and who am I to defy Him? We went inside, sat down, stood up when instructed by the court deputy, then the judge came in, began the trial, and sat down again.

Then, the shooters were brought in, one by one. They were all young, barely a couple of years older than I was. Yet now, their entire lives were ruined because of that one day—the one act driven by a lifetime of hatred. They had not only taken away the lives of their victims, but they had also destroyed their own chances at life. Their own livelihoods.

If only someone had sat down with them, talked to them, explained things—maybe they wouldn't have done this. If only they had come to a SALAAM meeting, maybe they would have seen Islam.

I looked at each of them, one by one. Any hate or resentment I had felt toward them was gone. It washed off me so smoothly, like dirt washed off by water. Instead, it was replaced by an overwhelming sense of peace. A calming wave of serenity overtook my heart, pushing away all other emotions. Regardless of what they had done, they were still people—people who weren't as blessed as I was.

Their defense attorneys started speaking, and I found out that all these boys were orphaned at an early age and spent their entire childhoods in foster care. Once they aged out of the system, they were left on the streets. Labeled hoods, they lived up to the title. Hopeless. Society had failed them, leading them to fail society.

They had no one to teach them right from wrong. And this is what they turned into. This is what I was trying to prevent with SALAAM.

I wanted to show people the potential they held. If these boys had seen that, if they had recognized a greater purpose to life, they would have set out to fulfill it, leaving no room in their hearts for anger or hatred.

I looked up at the ceiling, feeling immense gratitude toward Mom and Dad for raising me the way they did and always being there. Then I looked at Mike, grateful to him for taking me in when I had nothing and not giving up on me.

I looked around at all the victims. Among them were people I knew, like relatives of Mr. Hamid and Sheikh Omar, who had also been shot in the leg, and Walid, who was at the masjid that day and had gotten grazed by a bullet. All these people—elderly and young—were part of the masjid community and had gone through the same ordeal as I had. In their eyes, I could see the trauma, but I could also see something else. Peace.

Sheikh Omar came over to me with a smile. "Salaam," he said. Salaam. Peace. "Salaam," I replied, returning the greeting, customary to all Muslims. We sat down and waited for the hearing to begin.

The trial lasted for days. The judge wanted to hear every detail of what had happened. Things got heated at one point, and two attorneys had to be separated. Through it all, however, the defendants remained silent, their heads focused on their laps.

On the second day, the victims and witnesses were called up one by one to share their sides of what had happened. I was called up first.

"Muhammad Arshad, please come forward."

I proceeded.

"Please raise your right hand. Do you solemnly swear that this testimony you're about to give is the truth, the whole truth, and nothing but the truth?"

"Yes," I replied.

"Please have a seat."

I sat down, and the prosecuting attorney began asking me questions. They were very specific, and some I didn't know how to answer since I had passed out when the defendants were arrested. I answered as best as I could and left.

After days of questions and testimonies, each of the defendants pleaded guilty to all the charges pressed against them. The judge told us that we would all get a chance to confront them if we chose to.

I had started working on a speech the night before. When the big day came, I was scared. Up until this point, I had never addressed them directly in court, and I didn't know what it was going to be like.

When I was called up to speak, I took out my speech. But I couldn't read it; it just didn't feel right. I put it away and took a deep breath. I decided to speak from the heart and talk to them as people, not just recite from a piece of paper.

I remembered what my mom had told me: If someone says something bad about Islam, show them the real Islam. This was the whole reason for SALAAM. The shooting was the whole reason for SALAAM.

"What you did to me and to everyone in this courtroom is unforgettable. I don't know why you did what you did, and I never will, but that doesn't matter anymore. It's in the past. If there's anything I've learned over the past year, it's that you have to look at your past to build a stronger future. And although I know that was not your intention, you made me stronger. You made all of us stronger.

You tried to destroy our masjid, yet we built it better than before. You tried to separate us, yet we united even stronger. You tried to give Islam a negative reputation, yet we portrayed it in a positive way for everyone to see. But I'm not here just to tell you all of this because you already know it, and I am not here to tell you that I hate you for it, because I don't. Hate is not our way; it's not the way. I hate what you did, but I don't hate you. I forgive you. What happened is now in the past, and I want to help you change whatever perceptions of Islam you had before. Hopefully, no one—regardless of their religious affiliations—will ever have to go through what we went through ever again."

One of the defendants, Rob, stood up and smiled at me. "Thank you," he said. "And I'm sorry. I'm really sorry. I know you don't believe me, and I don't expect you to. Just know that we all are so sorry."

I nodded at him and sat back down. Sheikh Omar spoke next, his speech very similar to mine.

"Like Muhammad said before me," he began, "hate is not our way, it's not the way." He went on about how he loved them and that he was there for them.

Altogether, the defendants were charged with three counts of first-degree murder, eighteen counts of attempted murder, and destruction of private property. They were sentenced to life in prison with the possibility of parole. Two different felonies and one misdemeanor—all in one day.

I caught a glimpse of Rob as he was being taken away in handcuffs. He smiled at me and mouthed "thank you." I smiled back.

The next day was my birthday, and Mike agreed to spend the day in Pennsylvania. I was excited, but I also knew it would be a little nostalgic. I would spend the entire day with Ahmad, but I wouldn't go anywhere near my old house because I didn't think I was ready to face it again just yet.

I texted Ahmad to let him know that we were coming, and he was thrilled. When we got there, Mike and Brian waited near the car, and I knocked on the door. Imran answered, dapped me up, and said, "Assalamualaikum! How have you been? We missed you."

I smiled.

Imran had always been like an older brother to me. Then, Ahmad came out. "Heyy, what's up?" We hugged. I had spent my last moments of normalcy with these people. They had been there for me through everything, and I had learned so much from them. Imran went out to greet Mike and Brian and invited them inside. We all settled in the living room, and Ahmad's mom brought out tea.

Ahmad asked if I wanted to hang out in the Ridgmore courtyard, and I agreed. "It'll be fun, like old times." I asked Brian if he wanted to join, but he shook his head. "You go on," he said. "I know you want to see your friends. Seeing your old life again might be overwhelming. I'll just stay here." I smiled and followed Ahmad out.

We played basketball for a while, just the two of us, like old times. Then some friends showed up, and we caught up on the bleachers. It was hard for me, though, since the bleachers were where Maryam and her friends would always meet. They'd sit there, talking and watching us play, waiting for their rides home after school.

Maryam's best friend, Khadizah, who was also Ahmad's cousin, arrived. Ahmad told me that she had struggled with the loss and wanted to reach out, but didn't know how. We spent time talking, and it felt nice to connect with someone who understood. We had both lost someone we cared about deeply and were still learning how to cope.

"I miss her, I miss you too. After you moved, I lost you both."

"Bro, when she was gone, I lost part of myself."

"Sometimes, I keep looking around, thinking she'll meet me here after school, like always. But she doesn't. Realizing that, time and time again, is hard, bro. Wallah, it's so hard. How have you been coping?"

"I'm better than I had been, Alhumdulilah. I've been trying to make peace with it, you know? Writing and honoring her in any way I can."

She looked off into the distance. "You know, Allah says He doesn't burden a soul with more than it can bear. When she died, I started doubting that. But seeing you thrive with everything you're doing, mashaAllah, I guess it really shows that Allah knows us better than we know ourselves."

"Khadizah, healing isn't linear. Some days I'm on top of my salah, driven by SALAAM, honoring my sister's memory. Then, there are days when anything reminds me of her and I'm left in tears. Some days, I smile reading her journal, and other days, it hits me like a punch in the gut because I miss her so much. The key to grief is taking it one day at a time, talking about it whenever possible."

"It just feels like there are a million unsaid words. Things I wanted to tell her, but now I can't. Things I want to tell Allah but can't find the words. It hurts so much, bro. Sometimes I'm scared to love again. Scared to seek refuge in Islam. I'm scared of holding on to our memories, because they feel like pain now."

"Bro, I understand you, wallah. Therapy has been helping me navigate a lot of the same things. Maryam was special to me—she was special to all of us. Her memory doesn't deserve to be forgotten, so no matter how much it hurts, we have to keep it alive, okay?"

"You're right."

"You still have my number, right? You know you can always text me if you need anything. You were my sister too, bro, and I've missed all of you so much."

I told her about SALAAM and everything we were doing. "If you guys are ever in New York, you should come to a meeting."

Ahmad walked over to us. "Do you guys want to head back now? It's getting late."

We went back to his house and hung out for a while.

We didn't mention Maryam or my parents for the rest of the evening. Ahmad's mom, though I could tell she wanted to ask, didn't bring them up either. She smiled kindly and insisted we take some food with us for the drive back to New York.

On the way back, Brian and I kept talking about SALAAM and an upcoming Palestine awareness meeting we would be holding.

I was scheduled for my second session the next day and, surprisingly, I was looking forward to it. Looking back at the past had proven to be liberating.

The next day was Monday, and I was still trying to process the fact that yesterday had actually happened. It had felt so surreal, like I was glimpsing into the past. I needed it. My next therapy session was that afternoon. This time, Dr. Meyers talked about regulating emotions. But it was different from the SEL classes I used to sit through every year in school when I was younger. This time, it was about bigger, more intense emotions—about overcoming trauma, just like I was trying to do.

Dr. Meyers didn't treat me like a little kid; he treated me as an equal, and I greatly appreciated that. I told him about yesterday, and he said that it was good for me to look back on the past. "Look back and observe, but don't overthink it. Don't question every detail and decision," he advised. "There are so many what-ifs that may run through your head, and it can be agonizing to think of them. Remember, what happened already happened. It's in the past. No matter what you think you could have done better, you can't, because it's already done. Now, we have to think of the outcome."

He paused and asked, "You believe in God, right?"

I nodded. "Of course."

"Well, when God has something decreed, it will happen one way or another. We don't have any control over His will. All we can do is adapt, heal, and recover."

He continued, "There's a saying in Islam: 'What is meant for you will reach you, even if it is between two mountains, and what is not meant for you will not reach you, even if it is between your two lips.'"

He was right. As a servant of Allah, I owed Him unwavering worship. I had no control over the obstacles life had thrown at me. All I could do was say *Alhamdulillah* and adapt. I had to thank Him and heal. He would heal me. He only tested me because He knew I could handle it. If Allah believed in me, then who was I not to believe in myself?

I looked at Dr. Meyers and said, "I will get through this." It was a statement to him, but more so, a confirmation to myself.

"I know you will, Muhammad," he smiled. "Bro, I know you will."

Then, he made me write about my life right now—

about the good and bad things I'd gained after the Accident. I compared my lists and realized that, although there were more bad things than good, it didn't necessarily mean the bad outweighed the good. I realized that the bad had brought out so much of the good. Like how the shooting brought out SALAAM and how the Accident brought me to New York. These things didn't make the bad less severe because the pain was still excruciating, but they definitely helped.

I left therapy that day with a little more clarity. I decided that when I got home, I would attach my lists to my journal.

But when I got home, I was greeted by a dark apartment. Confused, I wondered why no one was home yet. I went inside, and suddenly, the lights turned on. Mike and Brian jumped out and screamed, "Happy Birthday!"

"What? But it was yesterday, and I thought we weren't celebrating since we already went to Pennsylvania."

"Yeah, but we didn't get a chance to celebrate with you over there since you were busy with your friends. So, we're celebrating now!"

As he spoke, Mike opened the fridge and took out a chocolate cake with *Happy Birthday Muhammad* written in blue icing.

"Wow! This is incredible, thank you!" I exclaimed. Then Mike lit the candles and told me to make a wish.

Since Muslims don't wish on candles, I closed my eyes

and made a *dua* instead: *Ya Allah, thank you for making this past year full of blessings. Please do the same for the upcoming year. Send me a sign that what I'm doing is right, and show me that my family is proud of me.*

I opened my eyes, blew out the candles, and we all sat down to eat.

After the cake was devoured, Brian went to his room and brought out a gift bag. Inside, I found a picture frame with the photo of Maryam we had used for the SALAAM brochures. Underneath the photo was a quote.

I lifted the frame and read the words, shocked. *"Sometimes, we work so hard and do so much that we forget nothing is permanent. This world is temporary. Our existence is temporary. The only thing that is permanent is God."*

It was a quote from Maryam's journal—the journal I kept hidden in my bookshelf, the journal that was the only way I felt connected to her, the only part of her I was able to salvage.

That journal was personal. When Maryam was alive, she wouldn't let me read it. She said it was her imprint on the world that could only be read after she was gone. She left it for me, and only me. And now, Brian had gone through it without my consent.

"Where did you get this?" I demanded.

"From your bookshelf. It was supposed to be a surprise."

"I searched for the quote and photo while Dad put

them together," he responded. "So, you're telling me that you went through my stuff without my permission, grabbed the only thing I have left of my sister, and just casually flipped through it?"

"Bro, I'm sorry. I just wanted it to be a surprise."

"You know, I was wrong. I was wrong to consider you my brother. I was wrong to consider either of you family. My real family is gone, never coming back. Why would you think it's okay to go through my relationship with them? I thought I could trust you, but I was wrong!"

I barged out of the living room, ran down the hallway, and locked myself in my room. My reaction felt overboard, but I wasn't thinking. I was hurt and angry, backstabbed by the people I trusted most. They had betrayed a trust I had just started to rebuild.

From the living room, I heard Mike talking to Brian. "I knew you meant well, but you still shouldn't have gone through his stuff. It's private. We're not supposed to look into his old life without his permission. We can only take what he gives us and offer support. He's been through so much already. The last thing we need to do is upset him further."

I thought about all that Brian had done for me, how he'd always been there. What I had done to him the day of the shooting was far worse than what he just did, and yet he still forgave me. He only took the journal because he wanted to help, to do something nice. In so many ways, he reminded me of Maryam. I felt guilty for getting so mad.

Brian knocked on my door and came in. We both apologized. Then I pulled out Maryam's journal and handed it to him. "For you, to read. Because I trust you, and I know she would too."

"Are you sure? I mean, would she be okay with it?"

"She was the whole reason for SALAAM. This journal showed me that, and as the co-founder, you have a right to know SALAAM's origins. I folded a couple of pages I don't want you to read."

He silently accepted it and smiled, promising to read it. Then, we returned to the living room together for more cake.

The next day, we had our first SALAAM club meeting after Ramadan. A small crowd showed up. It wasn't the usual crowd we hosted during Ramadan, but it was something. Most of the people there were young— teenagers and their younger siblings. The meeting was very casual. We had no set agenda, so we started talking about topics like peer pressure and acceptance. Mostly, people hung out in their separate groups and did their own thing. Snacks and drinks were served.

Most of the crowd was Muslim. They stayed for a while before leaving to pray and read the Quran. We had screens set up to maintain gender segregation after hearing complaints from older members of the masjid community about too much mingling between boys and girls. It wasn't considered appropriate for the masjid.

Samira and Aaliyah were trying to organize a game for the younger girls, while Brian and I were attempting to do the same for the boys. But it just wasn't working. Nobody seemed particularly interested. We decided to leave them to their own thing and regrouped with Ali and Samir.

"This isn't working," I said. "We need a game, or this will be the end of SALAAM."

"Yeah," Aaliyah agreed. "It was a lot easier during Ramadan, since so many people come to the masjid then. But now, we need to work extra hard to encourage people to show up."

"Yeah, we know that. But how?" asked Brian. "We can't even keep a group of young kids entertained. How do we do that with a large crowd?"

"I don't know, but we need to think fast."

"I know!" Samir exclaimed. "We can play Jeopardy. We used to do that all the time at the masjid I went to when I was younger, and I loved it as a kid. Let's do it here. They're probably familiar with Jeopardy from school, so they'll already know how to play."

"Yeah, that's a great idea. I'll go upstairs and get the laptops to set up for the boys. You guys do the same on the other side."

"Alright, I hope this works."

We assigned Aaliyah and a few other girls to manage the girls' side while we set up on the boys' side.

The games went really well, and the younger kids had a blast. Pretty soon, the older kids—and even some adults—joined in. People started forming teams and playing against each other. They were learning, but more importantly, they were having fun. Some of these kids probably thought those two things were mutually exclusive, but I proved them wrong. Islam proved them wrong.

We all went home that night in a great mood. Nobody seemed to want to leave, so we had lingered for quite a while. We made plans for a big Jeopardy game where boys would compete against girls, and the winning team would get a prize. It would take place in a month, and the kids were hyped.

"I think I should probably head home," I said after everyone had left and we finished cleaning up. "Assalamualaikum, everyone!"

"Yeah, we should all leave since it's getting pretty late," said Sheikh Omar. "Walaikumassalam."

The next few days were filled with Regents prep and AP exam recovery as exams were fast approaching, along with figuring out what kind of questions we would have at the tournament. Then Friday arrived. It started off like any other day—just as all days do. But I've learned to always expect the worst. I mean, the day my family died started off as a normal day too—only now, they're gone. From that day on, I became skeptical of the term "normal day." Every day starts out normal, but it's the outcome that matters.

I went to school as usual. The morning seemed to drag on forever, so I was grateful when lunch finally arrived. I raced to the cafeteria where my friends were sitting. As I checked my phone, like I usually do during lunch, that's when I saw it. A wave of rage overcame me as I processed what it meant.

It was an email from a major Islamic Relief organization that did humanitarian work around the world. They had asked me to be their ambassador. Alongside my friends, I would be flying out to various parts of Africa next month to help those in need. I was overjoyed, barely able to speak. Sam grabbed my phone to see what I was gawking at, and he had the same reaction: utter shock. I told Samir and Ali, and they were over the moon.

"This is it, guys! This is what we were working towards, Alhamdulillah!" exclaimed Samir.

The organization wanted to interview me next month and asked me to give a short speech on what I had seen and what I wanted to do to help. Things seemed to be moving so fast—I never imagined SALAAM would lead to something like this. Finally, I would be able to fulfill a purpose. Maryam had always wanted to do something like this, and now I was doing it in honor of her.

I texted Brian to share the news, and when we went home that night, we started making plans. First, we both had to get our regents out of the way. I had two exams the next day. We needed to finish the school year strong. Despite the whirlwind of events, I had maintained my grades, and I didn't want that to change.

We went to school early the next morning for regents. The time flew by as I put everything I had worked for into those exams. I felt confident that I had done well. Afterward, I caught up with everyone else, and they felt the same about their exams. Now that it was finally over, we had to focus on more important things. The next few weeks were filled with packing and mentally preparing for the journey. We put a hold on our weekly SALAAM meetings to fully concentrate on getting ready for the trip.

I told Dr. Meyers everything, sharing how excited I was, and he told me this was exactly what I needed. "Traveling like this at a young age will change your perspective on the world. Trust me, I went on a similar trip at your age, and I don't regret a second of it. It won't be a vacation—it's going to be physically and emotionally draining, but it's good, really good."

"I know," I said, smiling. "It's going to be one of the hardest things I'll ever do, but I can't wait."

A few days later, the five of us were on a plane with

Walid, Nouria, Auntie Jameela, and Mike. Many other volunteers were traveling with us. Our first destination was a small village in southern Sudan that was deprived of water and other basic necessities. The little water they had was contaminated, and the organization was working on digging wells for them, as well as distributing aid packages we had assembled at one of the SALAAM meetings with the help of the masjid.

It was a long journey, and we were all exhausted. When we arrived at the airport, we were surprised to find it small and almost empty. It didn't look like an airport, but more like an abandoned building. Our plane was the only one that had landed. Customs agents didn't give us any trouble due to our American passports, but something told me that if we were Sudanese citizens, the treatment would have been vastly different.

We had to take a bus to where we would be staying, but this wasn't the kind of bus any of us were used to. It was broken down, small, and cramped. What stood out to me about the weather in Sudan was how humid it was. The heat seemed to stick to the air, making it hard to breathe. It felt like a thick coating of mud that you had to struggle through—very condensed, seeping through your pores. Being tightly packed on that bus didn't help. We each brought only one duffle bag, but we still had trouble fitting everything on the bus.

"These mountains are so pretty," Ali pointed out. "Where are we again?"

"In the middle of nowhere," joked Brian.

The bus ride seemed to take forever, and I longed for it to be over so I could breathe real air.

"Bro, I can't believe we're done with school AND we now have something interesting to put on our college apps. A trip like this is bound to get us a free pass to Harvard," Brian said, trying to lighten the mood.

I tried to stay optimistic. "Let's hope we survive first before you all start dreaming of college," Walid retorted, and we all laughed.

We finally arrived at our "hotel," though I would hardly call it that. It was an old house in very bad shape, with two small rooms and a small bathroom near the entrance. That was the whole house. We split up accordingly, with Nouria and Auntie Jameela in one room, and us guys crowded into the room at the front. We laid a few old blankets on the bare floor and tried to fall asleep. Sleep didn't come easily, though. The loud noises and the thought of what these people lived through on a daily basis kept me awake. The constant attacks, the extreme poverty—it was hard, very hard.

The next day, we had to visit the refugee camp. We took the bus there again, bringing all the supplies to distribute. Handing out food, water, and blankets was so rewarding. It wasn't just about giving out basic necessities—it was about giving a ray of hope to these people. One little boy even came up to me and asked in broken English if he could take a picture. He looked at me the way someone would look at a celebrity. No, a hero. But I didn't feel like one. I just felt like I was doing something that needed to be done. If I didn't do it, then who would?

At first, I had dedicated myself to serving my community to honor Maryam and my parents, but now I realized I was doing it for something bigger. I was doing it for the sake of Allah. That shift in perspective, realizing I was serving a much greater purpose, acted as a source of motivation. It pushed me to work harder and exceed all my limitations.

I went on to further serve my people, my brothers and sisters, the ummah. We partnered with other organizations and did extensive humanitarian work across Africa. We expanded our social media platforms—SALAAM had over a million subscribers on YouTube and almost five million followers on Instagram. Our crowd was full of dedicated individuals looking to strengthen their faith and serve their community. Their drive was the same drive that had led me to initiate such a beautiful organization.

All across Africa, my friends and I were recognized. We attracted crowds in every country we visited. We dug wells in impoverished villages in Kenya and built masajid in Somalia. For a week, I sat in a masjid built by the generous donations of our followers and did my Islamic duty of giving dawah. I sat in front of a group of ambitious young boys, so much like I had been at their age, and helped them with their hifz journeys.

"Five years ago, I sat in seats similar to yours, eager to fill my heart with the words of Allah. Today, I am here to give you the same gift that I was given." I corrected their tajweed, helped them improve their pronunciation, and shared my love for the holy book with them. Their English was limited, and I knew no Somali, but with the words of Allah in front of us, no other words were necessary.

While my friends handed out aid packages across the village, I stayed in the house of Allah, absorbing the serenity of the sight, building an unbreakable bond with my younger Muslim brothers. They looked up to me in a way I had longed for someone to look up to me at their age. I was on the verge of tears when we departed. I hugged each one of them tightly, promising to return for their hifz graduation. One day, when they finished, we would recite together.

"InshaAllah," they all said in unison. InshaAllah. God willing. I looked forward to that day with all my heart.

CHAPTER 22

We had one more stop to make in Africa that summer—the one I was both looking forward to and dreading the most. We were going to Morocco. The last time I stepped foot in my home country, I was ten years old. My entire family had traveled there to reconnect me and Maryam with our culture, something that had been a prominent part of our lives since early childhood. Afterward, we went to Pakistan to see what it was like there. Although that trip is a blur in my mind, I vividly remember the sights I saw in Morocco—the intricate details in every building, the crowded open-air markets, the serene view of the ocean, and the fragrant smells of cooking that reminded me of my mother's kitchen.

But the thing that had shocked me the most was hearing Arabic spoken all around me. Although we lived in a relatively large Muslim community, there were few Arabs. All of my close friends were South Asian, and Arabic had always felt like a secret between me, Maryam, and my mom. Hearing it spoken in the streets made it feel like the secret was out—like we were exposed. Even now, as I inhaled the Moroccan air for the first time without my family, I felt that same shock at the sound of Arabic surrounding me.

Samir, Auntie Jameela, and I realized it was now our responsibility to translate every interaction for the group. The taxi driver made small talk with us, and I realized my Arabic was getting rusty. I no longer used it often, and he spoke in the Casablancan accent, which I wasn't very accustomed to. Samir, however, was chatting away, and Auntie Jameela chimed in occasionally.

"This sounds like gibberish," Ali remarked, rolling his eyes. He and Nouria spoke standard Arabic but didn't know the Moroccan dialect.

"What can I say? We're just like that," I laughed.

Once we got to the hotel, we were relieved to find it much nicer than what we had grown accustomed to during the trip. We had access to four separate rooms, and we split up accordingly. The rooms were well-furnished, and the structure was modern, providing a refreshing contrast to the preserved old buildings visible from the balcony. We had two days to enjoy the sights of Fes, a city known for its architecture and rich history. It was home to the world's first-ever Islamic University, founded by a Tunisian woman named Fatima Al Fihri. The university, Al Quaraouiyine, is still holding classes today. Walking there with my friends and family was nostalgic, and I reminisced about the first time I had visited. Maryam and I were amazed by the sight and insisted on taking pictures of everything—pictures we no longer have, memories that are now fading.

Mom had told me that my grandfather had attended that university for high school—the grandfather I had never known, with stories I had never heard. Mom didn't often talk about her childhood in Morocco, but she did for the first time on that trip, as the four of us sat closely together on the hotel room couch. Squinting in the dim light, I could see a happiness on my mother's face that I had never seen before. A glow that illuminated her the second she stepped foot on her homeland. They say you'll forever have a special connection to the place where your umbilical cord is buried, and I could see how true that was for her. She seemed so happy. So carefree. She radiated a special energy that was evident in her eyes.

Then I asked her, "Mama, what was it like growing up here with Mima and Ba Sidi? Why don't you ever talk about them?"

Her eyes fell for a second, but they quickly regained their glow. "Thank you for asking, my love," she said, smiling. "I don't bring them up because it makes me sad, but thank you for asking. You need to know. I grew up in Rabat, the capital of Morocco. Your grandparents, however, met in this beautiful city while your grandfather was studying at Al Quaraouiyine. He went there for tajweed classes and would always see Mima running errands at the grocery store nearby. Soon, he found out where she lived and went to her parents to ask for her hand in marriage. Shortly after they married, Ba Sidi served in the army for two years, and afterwards, they moved to Rabat, where they had me. Alhamdulillah, my childhood was full of vibrant culture and devotion to religion—just like our home is now."

She paused, then continued, "However, our extended family didn't approve of the modern approach my parents took in raising me. They didn't like that I wasn't expected to wear the hijab or dress modestly, and they hated that my parents didn't have any more children after me. Although I eventually wore the hijab and practiced modesty, our family didn't like the emphasis I put on religion over culture. I showed a great passion for Islamic education, unlike my regular studies. They expected my parents to maintain the same balance of culture and religion that they did. When we didn't follow through, everyone broke ties with us."

Her voice softened. "After my parents died, I had no idea what to do or where to go. My grandparents had passed away already, my aunts and uncles didn't care for me, so after the Janazah, I applied for a visa and came here, attempting to bury away any memories of Morocco. But after I got married and had you two, I realized I had the responsibility to keep our culture alive for your sake. So you'll know your past, where your ancestors came from, and so you can be proud of it. I want you to always remember this: faith and heritage make up our identities. You must always hold tightly to both of them. I will always be here to guide you, and when I'm not, Allah will be."

Maryam, Dad, and I listened in awe. None of us had ever seen this side of Mom before. Yet knowing it gave me a greater sense of assurance and confidence about my identity. I knew I would always take pride in both parts of my culture and display them to the world unapologetically.

Being in Morocco again reminded me of that. Seeing the university a second time with Sam, Samir, Ali, and Brian all goofing off together made me reflect on how quickly life can change. If I had been told a few years ago that I would be here today, I would have been overwhelmed with sadness. Yet, as I stand here now, the grief is still present, but I am happy and grateful for this moment.

After everything I witnessed this summer, I realized how much worse things are for others, and how privileged I am to have had the chance to help while also doing deep personal reflection on my life and identity. Back at the hotel, we braced ourselves to bid farewell to the luxury of the city and return to the harshness of village life. The next day, we crowded into a tightly packed bus headed toward the mountain villages, where some of my ancestors were from. The ride, which took two hours, felt like two days. I tried to journal, but my brain was fried, and nothing came to me. I closed my eyes, willing the trip to end, but waves of nausea overtook me. *Ya Allah*, I thought, *Let me get there in one piece.* Moroccan transportation was something I didn't miss.

Despite the exhausting trip, we passed the time talking and playing games. I was relieved when we finally got off the bus, but the sight that greeted me was surprising. The land was barren except for small mud houses and barns with animals roaming freely. Acres of olive trees stretched across the landscape, and sheds housed machines used for pressing olive oil—one of Morocco's prized exports. The village was a stark contrast to the intricate buildings of the city. The children wore simple, old-fashioned clothes—like something from the fifties—outdated, but normal to them. They greeted us with curiosity and anticipation, pulling Sam and Brian to the lake and explaining a game with wooden boats made of sticks. They spoke rapidly in a mix of broken English and Arabic. I laughed as Brian and Sam nodded, pretending to understand, their faces betraying their confusion. Ali and Samir joined us, with Samir translating.

I greeted the elders with hugs and a kiss on the forehead, a customary sign of respect in Moroccan culture. I had to introduce myself, which felt strange, as wherever I had gone lately, everyone seemed to know me. But in this secluded village, with no internet access, my being American came as a surprise. Not just American, but also a mix of Moroccan and Pakistani, a combination that was unheard of here. The younger kids thought of the United States as an almost mythical land where life was perfect—a dream they all wished to reach. I didn't want to burst their bubbles, but I felt the need to clear up their misconceptions. Allah created us all differently and allowed us to live in various parts of the world for reasons unknown to us. We must make the best of our situations. As I handed out care packages, I reminded them of this. They all smiled and hugged me.

"My loves," I said, "Allah has given you purpose here, just as He has given me mine elsewhere. Please serve it." Their gratitude touched me deeply, and I found myself reluctant to leave.

That night, the villagers hosted us in their homes. They were incredibly hospitable, serving their best food and offering their finest cushions and blankets. We spent the evening laughing, exchanging stories, and joking with the older village boys. They told us about their lives—tending to olive trees and sheep in the mornings, attending school in the afternoons. Most dreamed of moving to the city for college and pursuing careers afterward. Despite the hard concrete floor beneath me, I enjoyed that night far more than the sterile hotel in Fes.

The next morning, we said our goodbyes. It was our last day in Morocco, and I wanted to visit Rabat. I longed to walk the same ground my mother had walked at my age. The trip took four hours. We stopped in Casablanca to shop for snacks and souvenirs at the large market-place, eating sandwiches at a local restaurant and drinking freshly squeezed orange juice from a stand.

When we finally reached Rabat, the sea-scented air greeted us. The people in the capital were friendlier, and their Arabic was easier for me to understand than in the other cities. At the ocean, everyone hung around the boardwalk, but I kicked off my shoes and ran to the sand. Sorrow overwhelmed me again. I grabbed a fistful of rocks and threw them into the water one by one. I hated questioning Allah's will. After the therapy sessions I'd gone through, I'd found a relative sense of acceptance, but sometimes, I couldn't help but wonder, "Why? Why them? Why me? Why now?"

Why could I never hug my family again, never seek their advice, never ask for their guidance? Why did my mother's extended family not reach out to her? Why didn't I see glimpses of my mother in her relatives? Why couldn't I have her uncles, aunts, and cousins to embrace me, help me with my grief, reminisce about her life? Why did they not feel the same burden of sorrow I did? Was she not also their blood?

I dipped my feet into the water and washed my face. The water was cold, but it couldn't cool my burning heart. I began to cry—like I had in the library, like I had in my room on Eid. But this time, I was completely alone.

Nobody was there to comfort me—nobody but Allah. My tears mixed with the salty water. I made wudu with the seawater and prayed two rakats on the beach, my forehead covered in sand. Once I finished, I ran to my mother's childhood home, which was right by the ocean.

I stared at it for so long that I hadn't noticed Brian standing beside me, his arm over my shoulder. "Do you want to go in?" he asked softly, his hand resting on my shoulder. "If you ask, they might let you."

I thought about it and realized I might never get this opportunity again. We walked over to Mike to ask for permission, and once we had it, we returned. I knocked on the door, and an elderly couple answered. I introduced myself and asked if it would be okay to enter. They happily agreed.

The house was small but airy. Upon entering, the first thing that greeted us was a spacious courtyard. The couple had arranged a cozy seating area there. I could imagine my mom huddled on one of the large armchairs, a book on her lap, her glasses sliding off the bridge of her nose.

We then moved inside the house. A large, narrow hallway stretched before us, with rooms on either side. The first room was the bathroom, with a sink outside. I started to notice a theme of blue throughout the house. The courtyard had blue tiles, as did the concrete walls and floor. Even the couches in the guest living room were blue.

Next, I entered Mom's childhood bedroom. It was small, and the couple had turned it into another living room, but I could clearly imagine it as my mom's room: her desk piled with books, a closet full of clothes, and a bed pushed to the side. The elderly man noticed me lost in thought.

"It's good that you're doing this," he said. "Reflection is important. It's something we all need from time to time."

"It is," I agreed. "It really is."

He went into a closet and pulled out a brown box. "We found this here when we first moved in," he said. "I think you might want it." He handed it to me. On top of the box was the word *Sara* written in delicate Arabic calligraphy. I touched the writing and smiled.

"Thank you!" I exclaimed. "Wallah, thank you so much!"

The couple insisted we stay for tea. In a typical Moroccan household, guests are always offered tea before leaving. When we told them we were traveling as a group, they invited everyone inside. I clutched the box tightly, as if it might fly away. I promised myself I wouldn't open it until I was home, in the privacy of my room.

In the meantime, I drank tea and conversed with the kind older couple. Their grandson, who was around our age, had also joined us and was talking to Samir, who translated for the rest of the guys. Before we knew it, two hours had passed, and it was time to head to the airport. It was time to go home.

On the flight home, everyone was silent. But the silence was comforting. It felt like everyone was absorbing the past month and a half, trying to convince ourselves that it had actually happened, that the extraordinary events were real. We had left Africa better than we had found it. The difference was small, barely noticeable to some, but it meant the world to those living in poverty.

SALAAM had enabled so much—from changing non-Muslims' perceptions of Muslims to transforming the lives of Muslims. I was eager to see what more the organization would bring.

When we got home, we discovered we were on the front page of the New York Times. Several online news articles and blogs had been written about us. Our friend group was becoming almost as well-known as the organization itself. We were being called the teenage activists making a difference in the Muslim community.

CHAPTER 23

I spent the last week of summer mentally preparing for junior year, deciding what steps to take regarding SALAAM. I wanted to continue our weekly meetings, which were growing larger each week, but I also wanted to hold off on any bigger projects. Junior year is the hardest year of high school, and attending a school like Willow Heights wouldn't make it any easier. I needed to focus and work harder than ever to maintain my perfect GPA. I wanted to do well in school; it was the least I could do to make my parents proud.

Of course, I took the opportunity to open the box from the kind elderly couple. I waited for a day when Mike and Brian were both away from home. I locked the door, sat down on my bed, and began to open it. For some reason, my heart started racing. My hands began to shake uncontrollably, and tears pricked the corners of my eyes. I blinked them away, but eventually, I gave in and let them fall. Once again, I let myself release the sorrow—bit by bit, day by day. Dr. Meyers had said that healing wouldn't come quickly; it would take time, and setbacks were inevitable. My trip to Morocco had been a step forward, but it had also been a big setback. The time of reflection there had been nice, but returning home, I realized that it had also provided closure. Opening this box would solidify that fact. In a way, I'd be closing the door on any mystery or lingering questions about my culture and background, moving forward to something new.

I took a deep breath and opened the box. The first thing I saw was an old Polaroid photo of a young girl, about my age or possibly a few years younger, smiling. Her eyes were the same color as mine, and her smile was identical to Maryam's. She wore a light blue hijab and a white lab coat-looking jacket—the standard uniform for schoolchildren in Morocco. It was my mom, back when she was in high school. I kissed the photo and set it on my nightstand, promising myself I would buy a frame for it as soon as possible.

I reached into the box again and found another photo, this time of my mom as a baby. She had curly brown hair and rosy pink cheeks—she looked just like Maryam at that age. Her carefree expression and warm glow were unmistakable, traits she had carried throughout her life. The last time I saw her, she wore that same smile. The box also contained a few hair clips, a dress that I knew Maryam would have loved if she were still alive, and a small compact mirror. At the bottom of the box, I found a purple journal. I opened it and began to read. She had written in it every day, documenting her life, struggles, hopes, and dreams. I flipped to the last entry and began reading:

"Tomorrow is the day I will leave this life behind to start a new one. I will no longer feel the soil under which my parents rest. I will no longer inhale the air that strengthened me into the girl I am. I will no longer grieve two valuable lives lost; instead, I will grieve an entire identity lost. The Sara I am now will die tomorrow. A new journey awaits. New hardships, new people, and a new persona will emerge. I will not search for a family; I will create one. I will not let society shape my identity, but instead, I will build one of my own. I no longer see Morocco as the place that took my world away, but as the place that gave me life and an opportunity for a future. It is the land that holds the flesh of my ancestors and will forever hold my heart. The United States will be my home, but Morocco will be the home of my soul. When I find my life partner, no matter where his roots lie, I will ensure he respects my identity as a woman, holding firmly to the rope of my culture and to the rope of Allah. My children will look at Morocco as a land of reassurance, a land of familiarity. This journey is full of endings, but no ending is permanent. Its legacy remains alive in every aspect of one's life, as Morocco will remain alive in mine. The only permanent

ending is the akhirah; until then, every ending is simply a new beginning."

I held the book tightly to my chest, tears streaming down my face. Now I understood where Maryam and I got our love of writing from—and our deep sense of cultural pride. You did it, Mama, I thought, smiling. You did it right. She was right. There are no true endings in this world, only entries into new beginnings. The journal had several empty pages, where Mom must have intended to document her new beginnings. I smiled, deciding I would continue her story from here, as a symbol of her legacy.

The first day of school arrived, and Brian and I got back to our old routine of commuting together. As I entered the building and glanced at my schedule, a wave of dread overtook me. I had four AP classes and the rest were honors. I quickly made a dua and headed to AP Lang. The first day wasn't terrible. We made introductions, received our syllabi, and were assigned some reading. The rest of my classes were similar. The first day was relatively light, but I knew it wouldn't stay that way for long.

Afterward, I caught up with the guys to see how their first day went. Surprisingly, none of us had any classes together this year, which I found incredibly unfair. I was concerned that our brotherhood wouldn't remain as tight, but I pushed that thought aside. We did, however, share some teachers. All of us had Ms. Smith for AP Lang, and we concluded that a nice teacher might make the upcoming torture a little more bearable.

The first couple of weeks were slow but extremely rigorous. I was up every night until midnight finishing homework. Oftentimes, we'd all get on call to work together, waking each other up when we dozed off. Junior year had just begun, but we were already dying. I had to cancel two SALAAM meetings just to keep up with my work. If I continued at this pace, there was no way I'd be able to balance other aspects of my life. SALAAM meant so much to me, but already I was starting to neglect it. I needed to figure out how to organize my schedule better.

One day, in early October, I decided to talk to my guidance counselor about ways to balance everything. I thought about dropping one of my classes to have more time for the things I loved. Little did I know, school would soon become the least of my problems, and that decision would seem so minor compared to the calamity that was about to unfold.

CHAPTER 24

October seventh was the day. The date remained ingrained in my mind and in history. It was the day we heard the horrifying news that would change life for Muslims across the globe. Hamas, the political and military resistance movement in Palestine, had attacked a music festival in Israel. Several hostages had been captured, and people had endured serious injuries. Naturally, I couldn't help but sympathize with those who had to endure such pain. Yet, I knew that the pain of Palestinians was far greater, their suffering far more extensive for over seventy years. Now that they had decided to strike in an attempt to defend their land, the world would not remain silent. White privilege at its finest. No amount of Palestinian blood shed could compensate for Israel's suffering, apparently. Palestine would be under harsh attack by the Israeli government once more. Once again, they would be trapped in the world's largest concentration camp—also known as Gaza. Jerusalem, the holy land, was in further danger.

Being both Arab and Muslim, I have felt a strong connection to Palestine my entire life. I was raised with it; it had been ingrained into my mind since childhood. My biggest aspiration has always been praying within Masjid Al-Aqsa. The mosque holds great significance in Islam but is now under occupation. When I was younger, Maryam and I would talk about how we would one day go together and fulfill Allah's will by returning Masjid Al-Aqsa to the Muslims. We would be deemed heroes by the entire ummah, and we would be the first to pray there together.

"I am going to be the Imam," I would say.

"I am going to lead the entire ummah in Salah."

"No, I am going to," she would reply. "I am going to start hifz and memorize more than you."

I would laugh and remind her that, in Islam, women couldn't lead the Salah.

"But don't worry," I would say. "We can still make dua together afterward."

"InshaAllah," we would say in unison.

The weeks following were met with merciless attacks—attacks that Western media refused to portray. The photos and videos that I saw awoke in me a painful agony I thought had long been diminished. It ignited a feeling stronger than anger and hatred: a sense of vulnerability I thought I had already tackled. These mixed emotions left me weak—too weak to stand. I saw a sixteen-year-old boy screaming out in Arabic: "She's gone! She's gone and left me all alone. They took her from me," as he held the lifeless body of his sister. It reminded me of how I had felt a few months prior, though his trauma was greater than mine ever had been. We were the same age, and had lived the same amount of time, yet he had seen in sixteen years what I hope to never see in a lifetime.

He stood alone, amidst the scattered remains of people, smoldering debris, and crushed bricks from bombed homes. His sister was close to his chest as he knelt down, weeping. Then, suddenly, he stood up. What he did was extraordinary. He said, "Alhamdulillah. Praise be to God." The imaan of the Palestinians was special. It was something I would spend my entire life trying to attain.

Suddenly, I was exhausted, and I just wanted to go home. My entire body felt numb. My palms were sweaty as I clutched my phone tightly to my chest, seeing a photo of a young girl with her hair in two space buns. She had been martyred. She was being held in her grandfather's arms, his salt-and-pepper beard tickling her cheek. Reem. Her name was Reem.

When I got home, I wanted to talk to Dr. Meyers, so I scheduled an appointment with him for that afternoon. What I didn't know was how much the conflict was impacting the United States as a whole. The government supported Israel and would use taxpayer money to send aid. Our money was used to support murder. That realization provoked even more hatred within me.

Although Dr. Meyers tried to remain neutral and professional during our session, his views on the issue were clear. He had no sympathy for my side. For the first time, I left his office angrier and more confused than when I had entered. I told Mike that I no longer wanted to go to therapy, that I was ready to move on. I couldn't tell him why. Honestly, I was scared that Mike would have the same views as Dr. Meyers. I couldn't trust anyone who condoned such atrocities. I could never look at them in the same way again. A fight for Palestine is a fight for Islam. A fight for Gaza is a fight for humanity.

I was scared that everyone around me felt differently, that they thought the "war" was "complicated," that they saw the killing of innocent lives as justified, as self-defense. What did Reem do? What did any of them do? What made it okay for their lives to be horrendously taken by people who are so depraved that they held no feelings of sympathy or compassion? It was frustrating. So unbelievably frustrating. Why does no one understand? This wasn't like the shooting where I was able to jump straight into action, or even like the humanitarian work in Africa where just a few handouts would make a great difference.

I took out my journal and began to write. But what came out was unexpected. I found myself writing a poem.

Dear Prophet Muhammad,
If only they knew how much you mean to me,
And how deeply you impacted humanity.
If only they knew of the speech you once gave,
When you declared all humans equal—
Arab and Non-Arab, Black and White.
Yet, several years later,
Some still fail to see that you were right.
If only they listened when you praised and honored women,
When you said the best of mankind
Are those who are good to their wives.
Only then would they see
That when it comes to gender,
Islam promotes equity.
If only they saw how kindly you treated the poor.
You taught us never to let our neighbors go hungry—
Your heart was open,
As well as your door.
If only they knew how you cared for orphans,
How you watched them as they grew.
You told us to do the same—
To shelter and provide for children,
Even if they were not our own.
If only they knew of your radiance, of your Noor,
How you lit up any room you walked into,
And how you stood for peace,
Striving to avoid war.
If only they knew of the revelations brought down to you,

Of how the Quran was revealed on Mount Hira,
On the 27th night of Ramadan.
When Angel Jibreel came down and said Iqra!—Read!—
Right before the next dawn.
If only they knew of your illiteracy,
Of how you never learned to read,
Yet still spread the message of the Quran—
Ya Ummi.
If only they could have listened as you led each prayer,
As you raised your hands in Takbeer.
You showed the world that Islam is welcoming,
And that there is nothing to fear.
If only they could have witnessed all that you endured—
How the non-believers mocked you,
And threw rocks at your face.
Yet you simply said Salaam,
And gave them their space.
If only they knew about your love for this world—
For the animals, the flowers, the trees.
If only they knew how much you loved people,
How you taught us not to give in to discontentment and greed.
If only they knew of your Imaan,
Of how you devoted yourself to Allah,
Even in a world so cruel.
If only they knew of how patiently and strongly
You spread the message of Islam, Ya Rasool.
If only they knew the kindness you showed the young,
And the respect you showed the old.

If only they knew of your benevolence,
And how rarely you would scold.
If only they knew how you taught us
To look out for one another—
To always have each other's backs.
If we are ever in need,
We call out to our Muslim sisters and brothers.
If only they knew of your heart—
So clean and pure.
You always had the best intentions,
Making those around you feel loved and secure.
If only they observed the advice you gave,
How you listened intently,
And told us to be kind, caring, and brave.
If only they heeded the words of those who praised you—
The Sahaba who followed you and called you Al-Amin.
Then they would have seen you as trustworthy,
And steadfast in worship, Ya Matin.
If only they knew how it pains me
To see them drawing you, mocking you,
Calling you names.
If only they took the time to see
That all of your teachings were true.
As I learn more about you,
My love for you continues to grow.
If only they knew how Allah declared you the best of the best,
The last messenger, the final prophet.
And how all Muslims long to meet you

On the Day of Conquest.
Muhammad ﷺ, *the greatest to walk this land.*
Muhammad ﷺ, *the most extraordinary man.*
Your name, O Messenger, is the one I hold most dear.
Because of you, the Ummah has flourished for over 1400 years.
Muslims of all cultures and backgrounds stand together,
And it comforts me to know
That I have 1.9 billion brothers and sisters by my side.
You're the brother I never met,
Yet love more with each passing day.
You gave us the gifts of guidance, brotherhood,
And worship of Allah.
Thank you, Prophet Muhammad,
For showing us Islam,
For showing us the right way.

From,
Muhammad

I had never written poetry before, but I needed a special way to honor such a special man. He loves us so deeply, yet that love is so often overlooked. We are told to love him more than we love ourselves, yet we often forget him—his wisdom, his guidance. We could never truly reciprocate all that he has given humanity. He warned us of hardships and urged us to remain strong.

Already, a sense of tranquility overtook me. Together. One Ummah. One body. I closed my journal and went to pray two rakat, thanking Allah for solidifying this moment of realization and asking for His blessing in all that was to come.

Later, I opened the Seerah—the story of his life. Though I had read the entire book from cover to cover countless times, I spent the entire afternoon fully engrossed in it, amazed by the small details I once took for granted. I clung to every single word, every single quote, every single piece of advice—allowing it to heal my soul, feed my mind, and comfort my heart.

I wanted to continue writing, to reach a greater audience. I wanted to make my views clear. If that meant facing backlash, so be it. By now, I was accustomed to it. It didn't matter to me. I had survived the shooting, and in its wake, I felt invincible—like nothing and no one could ever break me.

The emotional toll of the past few years had made me immune to condemnation. I didn't live for myself. As a Muslim, I lived for Allah. I lived to serve my community. With every word I spoke publicly, I sought to honor my brothers and sisters.

Once again, I would do just that.

CHAPTER 25

The next day, the SALAAM crew gathered to film a video detailing our work in Africa. It was hard to fake optimism, and despite our efforts, the video carried a solemn mood. A sense of stillness lingered in the background. We worked for several hours but eventually gave up. None of us had the motivation to continue. We couldn't even pretend to be mentally present. Unsure of what else to do, I asked Brian to go ahead and post it, hoping for the best. We ended the meeting early, drained and disheartened.

I had created SALAAM in response to the shooting, as a way to honor my family. But now, I realized the organization needed a much greater foundation. SALAAM wasn't just a response to my personal pain; it was a response to the suffering endured by Palestinians since 1948. Everyone condemned the Holocaust, yet the Palestinian genocide was condoned under the guise of Israel's right to defend itself. Zionism was revered while our people were repeatedly harmed—and no one dared to speak up.

I picked up my phone and reopened Instagram. A flyer for a protest in support of Palestine popped up on my feed. I asked Mike if I could go. He was hesitant at first, but I reassured him that I'd be with the community and would leave if anything happened. Once I gained his approval, I texted the guys in the group chat. Everyone was in. I shared the flyer on the SALAAM Instagram story with the caption: *Hope to see all of you there, insha'Allah. One small step for us, but one giant leap for Gaza.*

I scrolled through my feed. It was flooded with reels showing horrendous murders, throbbing amputations, and deafening bombings. They were truly living in the world's largest open-air concentration camp. *Ya Allah,* I thought to myself, *please be there for them.* The West's response made my blood boil. Their so-called neutrality was revolting. Calling it "The Israel-Hamas War" instead of the Gaza genocide was a deliberate misrepresentation. Hamas wasn't the one being targeted—it was innocent civilians. If war were the true intention, it would have been fought differently. This was ethnic cleansing. They wanted to rid Gaza of its inhabitants, to erase Palestinians entirely. They wanted Gaza—*our* beautiful Gaza—under their control.

The next day, I walked to Central Park with my

keffiyeh tied around my head, turban-style, and a large Palestinian flag waving in my hands. Brian had made a sign with the popular slogan: *From the river to the sea, Palestine will be free.* Ali held another sign: *In our thousands, in our millions, we are all Palestinians.* The truth of that statement hit hard. We *were* all Palestinian. If not by blood, then by heart. Our connection to the Holy Land was unbreakable. The genocide affected all of us.

Sam and Samir waved flags alongside us.

"I hope we don't get in trouble for this," Sam blurted out. "But I think we should be fine together."

I walked with my head high, confident and determined. Having my friends by my side gave me strength and reassurance. We *would* not be moved. Gaza *would* be returned.

When we arrived, the park was packed. Protesters marched in unison, waving signs and chanting. We joined in:

"One, two, three, four! Occupation no more! Five, six, seven, eight! Israel is a terrorist state!"

"No more deaths, no more pain! Justice for Gaza we proclaim!"

We screamed at the top of our lungs, but my rage only grew. I had the urge to scream louder, to react bigger. I *had* to do more. The crowd swelled as more people joined—Muslims and non-Muslims, Arabs and non-Arabs. We stood together. Our fight was one. We were all seeking justice.

Soon, the police arrived. But the energy of the protest was electrifying, and my adrenaline had never been higher. I wasn't scared. We were simply exercising our First Amendment right—something no one could take away. Their freedom may have been stripped, but ours would not be.

We sat on the grass, spreading out towels. I pulled snacks and water from my bag, feeling lightheaded from chanting. Then, the protest leaders stood to address the crowd. Among them was a young woman named Fatima Mansour. She had been active in advocating for Palestine long before the recent retaliation, and her voice was unwavering.

"Seventy-five years," she declared, "we have watched the physical and emotional deterioration of our people. Seventy-five years, they pleaded for help. Seventy-five years, we shed tear after tear, sent plea after plea. And yet, the public remained silent. They refused to expose the lies and hypocrisy Israel fed the West. They refused to acknowledge that our hard-earned tax dollars fund the slaughter of our brothers and sisters. But now, their lies have been exposed. Their crimes are in plain sight. And yet... some still choose to look away."

I am here to tell every one of you that it is now our turn. Our turn to refuse. We will refuse to succumb to their narrow-minded views on how we should perceive a tragedy that is far from political. We will refuse to succumb to their double standards on which lives do and do not matter—because, once again, all lives matter.

Our children deserve to live. Our people deserve to live. The people of Gaza are our family. Although their blood does not flow through our veins, their pain and sorrow remain ever-present in our hearts.

She dropped the microphone and stepped away. Her face was visibly distressed. She looked physically and emotionally exhausted. The sadness in her eyes mirrored the sadness I had seen in the eyes of the Palestinians. Yet, beneath that sadness, glimmered an undeniable hope—hope that was evident in everyone present. Hope for a better future.

She was an amazing speaker—passionate, articulate, and powerful. I wanted to speak like that. I wanted to be able to stand before a crowd and say, with conviction, that I gave it my all.

The microphone was being passed around.

"Muhammad, you should go," said Samir.

"Yeah, let the SALAAM guy speak," a random voice chimed in.

The next thing I knew, everyone was chanting my name, urging me to take the mic. And so, I stood up.

"How many people need to die before we get a response? How many children need to be orphaned before we receive even an ounce of sympathy from the American government?

The weight of being a so-called American is too much

to bear because of the hypocrisy and double standards imposed by a government that is supposed to protect ALL its citizens. Where is that protection for the thousands of students—students not much older than I am— who are sacrificing their well-being, their education, their futures for the sake of humanity? Where is the protection for students simply attempting to exercise their First Amendment right to freedom of speech, yet being silenced by the very law enforcement meant to protect them?

Because freedom of speech is only applicable when it aligns with their narrow-minded, prejudiced, discriminatory, and inequitable views—views that blatantly state: all lives matter unless you are Palestinian.

Your life doesn't matter if you are a Palestinian father clutching his young son, screaming, 'Ibni! Ibni!'—'My son! My son!'—only to watch him be killed by the heartless, bloodthirsty, brutish souls of the IDF.

Your life doesn't matter if you are a five-year-old Palestinian girl, lifeless in your grandfather's arms.

Your life doesn't matter if you are a ninety-two-year-old Palestinian grandmother, burned alive under the cruel hands of the state of Israel.

A region that is not a country, but a piece of stolen land. Land taken with great brutality—forcing its residents out while condoning those who robbed them of a home, of livelihood, of security.

Where is the healthcare necessary to heal our students

who have been injured while protesting? Oh right—our hard-earned tax money is in the hands of the Israeli government, transformed into bullets and bombs to kill our brothers and sisters."

I paused, allowing the audience to absorb my words. After a round of applause, I continued.

"The Holocaust continues to be spoken about, continues to be portrayed, continues to be condemned. Yet, the ongoing genocide is still called a war. A war where the oppressed side has no army.

The government I once hoped to work for has shown no remorse, no empathy, no consideration for my beliefs, for my voice. Where is the power of the people? Where is the voice of the people? Where are the so-called core values of this so-called democratic country that claims to have its citizens' best interests at heart?

They have us all trapped, making us think we are unable to move, unable to act.

But we, as an ummah, refuse to submit to them and their enraging, illogical claims. We submit to Allah, and Allah alone. We refuse to let their harsh, cold demeanors freeze our hearts and desensitize us. Instead, the warmth of our character will one day shine through, allowing us to witness a free Palestine.

The ummah is one body. When they hurt, we hurt. When they bleed, we bleed. When they cry, we spend nights weeping, calling out to Allah, begging for His mercy.

That is the beauty of Islam.

Our pain is one. Our suffering is one. Our struggle is one. Our fight is one.

Our fight for a free Palestine is one.

It is a dream we will meticulously strive for every single day. It is a fight we will devote our entire existence to. It is a fight we will fight with resilience. With dignity. With tenacity.

We will fight endlessly, with no respite.

We will not fall—we will lean on one another. We will not break—we will build one another up. We will not be cut—we will mend one another.

And as they burn the Palestinian flag, our very flesh burns along with it."

Our hearts ache for the blood you shed. Our eyes cry for the purity they have been robbed of. Our hearts ache for the ground our Prophet walked, for the masjid our Prophet prostrated in. Our hearts ache for the land Allah promised us, for the salah in Al Aqsa that we are deprived of. But our souls rejoice for the reward that awaits you in the highest level of Jannah—the reward of your sabr, ya ahl Falastin. The fruit of your labor, oh people of Palestine.

My brothers and sisters, our family in Gaza, have passed their test. Their akhirah will be full of ease, for they have endured the unimaginable in this dunya. Now, Allah is testing us. He is testing us through their struggle. He wants to see if we are worthy of being members of the greatest community to ever exist—the Ummah of Muhammad (saw). He wants to see if we truly are the best nation brought forth to the people, if we genuinely command the good and refuse to enjoin in evil. If we will stand up for what is right, even in unprecedented circumstances. If we will stand for our brothers and sisters in Islam, even when the entire world is against us.

The Palestinians have taught us so much about what it truly means to be Muslim. They have exemplified faith and restored belief in the deen. From reciting the Quran to ease unfathomable pain to thanking Allah after their relatives have been martyred—their imaan is remarkable. They are the kind of Muslims we should strive to be. They are walking examples of the Quran and Sunnah, living proof of Allah's qudrah.

As we sacrifice our comfort to ease their suffering, we should strive to be like them. We should learn to hope as they do, learn to rely on prayer as they do, learn to believe as they do, and most importantly, learn to love as they do. Because I can guarantee you, there is no one on this earth today who loves as deeply as our Palestinian brothers and sisters.

I want to reciprocate this love. I want to show them that they are worthy of it. I want them to stand with me on the Day of Judgment and intercede for me. On the day when they will be exalted and the rest of us will remain vulnerable, I want Reem to say that we grieved her death as if she were our own sister. I want Hind to say that we cried and spoke out for her with everything we had. I want Muhammad, Tala, Mays, Ahmed, and Farah to say that when the world was silent, we were not. When the world silenced them, we became their voices. We were their source of ease following hardship, their source of strength to keep going.

I want crossing the sirat to be easy for all of us, just as it will be for them. I want their souls to return to Allah at ease, knowing that their brothers and sisters on this earth are still fighting for them, crying for them, and sharing their legacies with the world. We can't rely on the government. We can't rely on our so-called fellow Americans. We simply can't rely on the hearts of those who have none. We can't rely on the empathy of those who have none.

When Biden says, "An attack on Israel is an attack on America," we say, "An attack on Palestine is an attack on Islam." Because a fight for Gaza is a fight for Islam.

Thank you.

The crowd fell silent for a few seconds before erupting into another huge round of applause. I smiled and sat back down. My friends were all awestruck, just like the day of the Quran competition.

"Bro, you ate that up," said Ali.

"Yeah, for real," replied Sam. "That was fire."

"Thanks, guys."

I received many more compliments from the crowd. A lot of people recognized me from the work I do and told me it was incredible. I thanked them and tried once again to process how everything had happened so fast.

After the chatter died down, someone else rose to take the stage. She looked oddly familiar. After a moment, I realized it was Aaliyah, the girl from my school. It turned out she had also played a part in organizing the protest, which was now turning into a gathering.

"Assalamualaikum and good afternoon to everyone," she began, greeting both the Muslims and non-Muslims in the crowd.

After we responded with "Walaikumassalam," she continued, "I want to start by thanking you all for being here and for understanding that we are here for a reason much greater than ourselves. We are here with a grief greater than our struggles. We are here to prove to ourselves and our community that nothing can hold us back from speaking the truth. Nobody will prohibit us from aiding those who are suffering. The pain they are enduring is, inshaAllah, a pain we will never have to know, but it is a pain we must fight to combat. Their fight is a fight we must strive to honor."

I want to honor them by performing a spoken word that I have written—not just for our Palestinian brothers and sisters, but for the entire Muslim ummah.

One ummah, one body.
United under Islam and its brotherhood,
Yet so many parts are consistently overlooked.

*Kuntum khaira ummatin ukhrijat linnas—our nation is the
best of the best.
We are those who will be saved on the day of conquest.
Though the one who once guided us is gone,
He left us his teachings—
And each other to lean on.
Want for yourself what you want for your brother.
Never let go of one another.
The Prophet told us to hold on,
Yet we are breaking all our ties,
Choosing to ignore the sorrow
In every Palestinian child's eyes.
You're scared to help your own people
Because of the harm that may come to you—
Yet you claim to be a Muslim?
Where is your virtue?
Allah entrusted their burdens to us,
Yet you leave them and break their trust.
You remain numb and desensitized,
While the worst possible genocide unfolds before your eyes.
Look at the land of Gaza—its history.
Every Muslim dreams to one day walk its soil,
Breathe in its air,
And witness it be free.
Together, we will walk to the beautiful Al-Aqsa Mosque,
Just as our Nabi did before.
He began the journey of Israa and Miraj
With two rak'ahs inside, remembering Allah.*

*His forehead touched the Al-Aqsa ground as he prostrated in
sujood.*
Yet you want to see it gone?
Your ideologies are so misconstrued.
His feet touched the Al-Aqsa ground
As he rose to the heavens above.
He led all of the anbiyaa in salah—
All those who came before his time.
Muhammad ﷺ up front,
The other mursalin behind.
Then he descended back
To the city every Muslim should call home.
Yet we let the Palestinians fight for it—
Alone.
I want to pray there one day,
Alongside all of you.
I want to ease the suffering of the ummah—
The Palestinians too.
I want to walk the ground
That our Prophet once did,
Feeling the soil beneath my feet.
I want to stand in the land
That once held the souls of our anbiyaa.
We cannot accept defeat.
I want to place my forehead
Where our Prophet placed his,
Bowing down in long sujood,
Thanking Allah for all He has given me—

For how He helped us overthrow
Those who dared intrude.
They thought they were strong,
But they had it all wrong.
They can't break a nation
That does not fear death.
For even as Palestinians take their final breath—
Even in times of unrelenting pain—
They still know that Allah is closer to them than their own
jugular vein.
We are one body—strong and united,
Looking to our Creator for mercy, hoping to be guided.
There is little we can do, this I know,
But Allah has promised us victory, so to Him we must go.
A Tahajjud du'a is never neglected—
Pray sincerely, and Allah will accept it.
We must fight for them in this dunya and keep them in our
minds,
For the Ummah is one body, and our fates intertwine.
InshaAllah, a day will come when our prayers are answered,
And together, we will stride
To a land we can call ours—with honor and pride.
But as we walk, we will see that it is no longer the same,
For Gaza has endured unimaginable pain.
The soil, once soft beneath our feet,
Will be hardened—mixed with bones, bullets, and concrete.
The rivers that once ran cool and crystal clear
Will be filled with Palestinian blood, sweat, and tears.

The buildings and houses that once stood tall and proud
Will have crumbled—shattered to the ground.
The laughter and joy of young children will be gone,
And in the air will linger a sorrow centuries long.
Yet, when you look up at the Gaza sky,
You will sense each shaheed passing by.
In the highest level of Jannah, they now rest,
Their sweet-scented souls lingering in the air—so fragrant, so blessed.
Alhamdulillah, Allah has ended their pain,
In Jannatul Firdaus, they will forever remain.
I look forward to the day I return to that land,
And when I do, I have a plan.
I will take the names of each martyr and write them on the country's ground,
A tribute to those who died so we could still be around.
I will dedicate my life to those who fought for me,
Not giving up the holy land, so future Muslims will see.
By the will of Allah—so pure and divine—
I will sit there, filling the land, line by line.
And as I do, I will weep tears of sorrow and shame,
For I could have done more to ease their pain.
Islam teaches us to stand for one another,
Our Prophet declared us all sisters and brothers.
Yet, my hands remain stained—the crimson red of Palestinian blood.
Surely, I could have done more to show them honor and love.
I will carry their legacies wherever I go,

And as I walk to Masjid Al-Aqsa, I will let the world know.
I will tell their stories—the pain none of us could fathom—
Writing out the names of Mahmoud, Sham, and Adam.
Young children, filled with hope and ambition—
They lived hard lives and deserve recognition.
I will write out Reem, a young girl with dreams,
Her hair in two space buns, her mind bursting at the seams.
She was the soul of our souls,
And I will spend my life making her story known.
I will witness the rebirth of a once-beautiful nation,
Its people's legacies rising—refusing obliteration.
I will write out Ahmed, Tala, Mays, and Farah,
Fatima, Hisham, Sila, and Ali,
Heba, Wafa, Hasan, Obaida, and Douaa too—
Every name, I will write, every soul, I will remember.
Even if it takes my entire lifetime,
I will stay there—it's fine.
For from the day I was born to the day I die,
I will forever stand with Palestine.

"Jazakumullahu Khairan and thank you all so much." She put down the microphone, leaving half the crowd nearly in tears.

"Takbeer!" someone suddenly shouted.

"Allahu Akbar!" we all responded in unison.

The response to the takbeer caught the attention of passing pedestrians. Fear flickered across their faces, and soon, an angry mob had gathered in front of us. People started yelling and cursing. My friends and I huddled in the back, watching the chaos unfold from a distance.

The police arrived.

"Alright, guys, break it up before we have to break you up."

"Yeah, we don't want a riot."

"There is no riot here," someone argued. "We are protesting an act we deem unjust. It's our right and our civic duty to speak out."

As Aaliyah walked away, clearly shaken by the unfolding events, a middle-aged white man approached her from behind. He crept up slowly, and my stomach flipped as I realized what was about to happen.

"Aaliyah!" I screamed. "Watch out!"

But it was too late. He had already yanked off her hijab.

Her face looked stricken and vulnerable, her eyes glistening with tears. She reached up to snatch it away from him, but he held it out of her reach. I averted my eyes immediately, realizing she was uncovered. She pulled her hood over her head, and I heard her start to sob.

Suddenly, a surge of anger overtook me. I looked over at her and saw Maryam. My younger sister had the same look on her face the day her hijab was pulled off. If I had failed as a brother to Maryam, I would not fail as a brother to Aaliyah.

I ran over, grabbed her hijab from the ground, and handed it back to her. Then I turned to the man.

"Hey, what the hell is your problem? Do you not realize what you just did is a hate crime?"

"There are too many of you here," he spat back. "The disease has already spread to Israel, and I won't let it spread here too."

"Are you kidding me right now?" I was furious. "You don't ever touch a Muslim girl. You don't ever lay your damn fingers on a Muslim girl. Understand? The only disease here is your prejudiced mindset. The only terrorism I see is what Palestinians are enduring. And you have the audacity to pull off her hijab? You attack her and still call her a terrorist? Proof, firsthand, that white privilege is real. I'll have you know something—our women hold value, and that hijab you just pulled off is a crown of Islam. I'm not about to let some creep like you disrespect my Muslim sister."

I charged at him, fists clenched, ready to make him pay. To make all of them pay.

Aaliyah stopped me.

"Muhammad, thank you. I really appreciate you standing up for me like that. I don't know what I would have done without you. But resorting to violence goes against everything you, SALAAM, and Islam stand for. Remember, hate is not our way. It's not the way. You said so yourself. Bro, you said it in court. Please, act upon it."

I exhaled sharply, unclenching my fists. We walked away together, but I still threw daggers in the man's direction with my eyes.

Where were the police now? They had been eager to break up our protest, but now, when we needed them, they were nowhere to be found.

"Are you okay?" I asked Aaliyah. "Like really, are you?"

"I'm fine, alhamdulillah."

"Alhamdulillah. Now, let's find a police officer and report this guy."

The report was made, and justice was served. But the passion we felt for our cause only grew stronger. After what happened to Aaliyah, our determination intensified —so did our fear. But the fear was nothing compared to the exhilaration.

CHAPTER 26

The events of the protest had left me shaken, but they only fueled my passion to work and speak out even more. For months, I kept writing, posting on social media, and attending protests. I jumped at any opportunity to speak the truth, even if it meant being singled out and targeted. My work brought me more recognition than ever before, and support for SALAAM soared—it was incredible to witness.

Aaliyah, however, was visibly shaken. After the protest, she completely stopped openly sharing anything. She became more reserved, barely speaking at school. She traded her long abayas for oversized hoodies, trying to blend in as much as possible. It broke my heart, but after what she had been through, her fear was understandable. She repeatedly thanked me for standing up for her that day. I told her, *"When you're ready to share your story, the world will be ready to listen, okay? Just like they listened to me, we will make sure they listen to you."* We had to have each other's backs and stick together. *One ummah. One body. Right?* Seeing her slowly start to heal brought me relief beyond words.

The best way to help one another, though, was through dua. Talking, begging, and pleading with Allah to ease their pain brought comfort to my heart—and hopefully to theirs. The day Israel cut off Gaza's water supply, Allah sent them rain. His mercy was so abundant, so visible. The people of Gaza, the entire Muslim ummah, had Allah by their side. With that kind of power, we were invincible. No soldier's shield could compare to the protection we had.

Waking up for tahajjud—being personally invited to spend that time with Allah—was an honor. The cold water dripping down my face as I made wudu startled me awake. The long sujood I bowed for on the prayer mat brought me indescribable ease. I would lay my hardships before my Creator, ask Him for guidance, and time after time, He would deliver. We were taught in the masjid that a dua made during tahajjud is never neglected. One way or another, Allah always answers. For the longest time, I thought that couldn't apply to certain dreams and aspirations. But Allah proved me wrong. After years of tahajjud, He made my biggest dream come true.

With His blessings, I was invited to visit Africa once again. This time, my destination was Egypt. Egypt bordered Palestine, and aid trucks were frequently sent from there, but the need for supplies was dire. An organization called Aid Gaza had several relief sites, and they requested our help assembling aid packages. I planned to use some of the SALAAM donations to purchase supplies. The urgency was high—any moment, the Israeli government could block access. The level of control they had disgusted me. How could such monsters be allowed to wreak havoc? Yet the world didn't see them as monsters. They saw them as victims.

I made the trip in the middle of exam season. I was so busy that I barely studied, relying heavily on my prayers to get me through. There was too much to remember and too little time. Exhaustion weighed on me, but through it all—eating, sleeping, studying—Gaza never left my mind. Long hours were spent on my prayer mat, Quran on my lap, searching for answers.

The moment my last exam was over, I rushed home, packed a small duffel bag with just a few changes of clothes and basic essentials, then headed to the airport, thanking Allah for the opportunity. This time, I would be traveling alone. My friends couldn't come—they were tied up with school commitments. By now, we were so used to doing things as a group that the thought of going without them left me a little sad. But for me, Palestine was my priority.

I moved through airport procedures quickly, never once feeling anxious about traveling as an unaccompanied minor. The plane ride felt slow, a heavy sorrow filling the air. We were given volunteer vests—identifiers meant to keep us safe as outsiders. Upon arrival, there was no time to check into a hotel, no moment to rest or drop off our bags. We went straight to the Aid Gaza site and began assembling packages.

The supplies had arrived beforehand—truckloads of flour, fruit, oil, tea, rice, shampoo, soap, and other non-perishable necessities filled the room. We pulled out stacks of empty boxes, filling them with enough supplies to sustain families of six for several months.

As I worked, I longed to feel Palestinian soil beneath my feet. My lungs ached for Palestinian air. My heart yearned for sujood in Al-Aqsa. I couldn't come this close and not fulfill such a dream. So once again, I turned to silent dua. *Ya Allah, return Masjid Al-Aqsa to the ownership of the Muslims.*

For days, we filled box after box, hour after hour. The work was repetitive and exhausting. At times, I thought I might die of boredom. But every time I closed my eyes from fatigue, I saw Reem—her eyes, once bright with innocence and hope, now shut forever. The image brought tears to my eyes, sorrow to my heart. And in her eyes, I saw Maryam's, urging me to keep going.

That thought alone was enough to keep me moving. Because if I stopped, who would save the next child?

Once the boxes were packed, we had to load the trucks. Along with the other volunteers, I lifted box after box, my heart feeling slightly lighter with each one. We handed over a folder of documents that would permit the items to cross the border into Rafah, and soon, the trucks were ready to go. They would be sent out in a few hours.

Before that, all the volunteers gathered for lunch. Shawarma wraps and cans of Egyptian orange soda were passed around. As we ate, we talked. The volunteers varied in age and came from all over the world. An elderly, newly widowed man was here in honor of his late wife. A group of college students wanted to give back to the community. And I—well, I was here for reasons that were clear yet oddly unexplainable.

We were all united by the same purpose: to aid those who were suffering, to give back to the ummah. To somehow ease a pain that was unfathomable. For some of us, it was about fate; for others, it was simply about humanity.

Despite the weight in our hearts, we found comfort in each other's company, sharing lighthearted jokes.

"Hey Muhammad, how old are you?" asked Farooq, a college student in his early twenties.

"I'm sixteen."

"Aww, guys, Muhammad is the baby of the group!"

Everyone laughed, including me. We got along so well that I hadn't even realized I was the youngest. I enjoyed the companionship of my new friends.

Soon, our short respite came to an end, and we decided to take a walk to the marketplace to see if we could buy fresh fruit to add to the trucks. Egypt was vibrant, and the marketplace was packed, similar to the ones in Morocco. Loud music clashed with the sound of the Quran and the rapid Arabic spoken by locals. Their dialect was vastly different from the Moroccan one, and I found it fascinating.

"This place is huge," a girl in our group remarked.

"I just hope none of us get lost," someone else said.

After asking for directions, we finally found a vendor. Fruit had become a scarcity in Gaza, and whatever little we could send would be greatly appreciated. Seeing videos of young children fighting over rotten bananas and apples broke our hearts. Something we often threw away without a second thought was a rare treat for them.

We bought several bags of oranges from a vendor, but as soon as he heard they were for the relief efforts in Gaza, he refused to take a single penny.

"It's for our brothers and sisters," he said in a thick accent. "It's the least I can do."

The generosity of the Egyptian people warmed our hearts. We thanked him and went to buy apples and pears from another vendor. By the end of our trip, we had gathered a decent amount of fruit to add to the trucks. It wouldn't be enough to revive Gaza, but maybe—just maybe—it would be enough to make a difference. Perhaps it would ensure that some children wouldn't have to go to bed on an empty stomach. That thought alone eased my worries, if only slightly.

We packed everything up, and soon, the trucks were ready to go.

But I couldn't let them leave.

Not without me.

No wasn't an option. This was what I wanted—what Maryam had wanted. I wasn't thinking rationally, but at that moment, all I could think about was how wrong it felt to be so close to such a huge dream, yet so painfully far. Within its reach, but just beyond its grasp.

The trucks would enter Jerusalem, but not Al-Aqsa. People would gather for prayer outside the masjid but be forbidden from entering—denied the comfort of such a sacred place. So close, yet so far. They were deprived of a land their ancestors had fought for.

We all were.

If I wasn't allowed inside, I wanted at least to witness the masjid's glory from the outside. To breathe in Gaza's air. And if I died in the process—so what?

I would be buried in the same ground that held my brothers and sisters—the martyrs of Palestine, the lights of the ummah.

Joining them would be a tremendous honor.

I asked the organizer for permission to ride along into Gaza and help distribute the packages. But my request was denied—I had to be over eighteen and provide specific documentation, which I didn't have.

"It's just too dangerous, Muhammad. I know you want to go in there—wallahi, we all do—but now is not the time. We can't take any risks. InshaAllah, one day, when Palestine is free, we'll all be able to enter with no questions asked. But today is just not that day, okay?"

"Yeah, I understand."

That was when I got the idea—something reckless, something that could put me in grave danger if it failed but in enormous trouble if it succeeded. None of that mattered, though. Not life. Not death. All I cared about was the feeling of serenity in Al-Aqsa, in Jerusalem. And even though I knew gaining access was nearly impossible, I at least wanted to be close.

The idea came in a split second, and I acted on it just as quickly.

I waited until everyone had gone inside to gather some forgotten supplies. Once I was alone, I climbed into the back of the last truck that hadn't yet departed and hid behind the boxes. My heart pounded as I held my breath, listening to the voices outside, the last-minute logistics being discussed. Then, Jamal—the truck driver—hopped in along with a few volunteers, and we took off.

We stopped at numerous checkpoints, and each time, my heart nearly stopped with us. The road was bumpy, the drive slow. But once we crossed the Rafah border, I finally let out a breath.

I was hot, sweaty, and cramped in the back of the truck. The only thing I had with me was my backpack, stuffed with a few possessions—my phone, passport, wallet, some extra clothes. And, of course, my journal.

I took it out, flipped it open, and, in silence, began to write.

Gaza's Ground

By: Muhammad Arshad

If you were to put your ear on Gaza's ground, you would be able to hear countless stories that have been left untold

*You would heed the screams and agony of all those young
and old
Gaza's soil holds pain, tears uncried, the flesh and bones of
those who had died
Leaving behind their families husbands and wives
Giving up their lives
For their land, and faith, submitting themselves to the mercy of
an apartheid regime
Fighting a battle with more roots than may seem
Holding on to their culture and deen**
*Their suffering still remains unperceived
If you were to place your feet within Gaza's soil, you will feel
the bullets, the moist sensation of crimson red blood, the
remains of the Palestinian flag buried deep within
The sorrow which they have become so accustomed to, for us
seems so foreign
No longer do we feel remorse or chagrin
Rather we have simply lost all emotion
Failed to get out the notion
That we are living during the time of a genocide
If you were to drink from Gaza's river
You would taste the metallic taste of the Palestinian blood
Mixed in with remains of bullets and bombs, people who know
the true definition of love
Have been separated and later berated
Their remains flow within the deepest recessions of their rivers
and seas
Year after year the world ignored their pleas*

If you were to inhale the Gaza air
Your lungs will be polluted with the residue of bullets and
bombs
The atmosphere uneasy and no longer calm
Your nose would be enchanted by the sweet scent of the martyrs
and their sacrifice
Yet the smell will not be enough to suffice
The loss of their blissful smiles
The sorrow extends for miles upon miles
Knowing no respite of such an emotion
So many of Gaza's stories remain unspoken
If you were to bestow your gaze onto the eyes of a Palestinian
child
You would find a river of unshed tears
A shield guarding their pain and fear
Strength embodied by the strongest people known to mankind
Devotion to a land whilst holding on tightly with pride
If you were to look up at the Gaza sky amidst the bright
sunlight and clouds
You would feel the sensation of smiles beaming down on you so
proud
Of the land they cried for
Died for
And prayed for to be free
A land with more value than many could see
If you were to peer into Gaza's homes and tents
You will cry tears of regret
Since you didn't try hard enough to prevent

The obliteration of a nation
Once so beautiful and abundant
The fight for Gaza was incumbent
Yet the oppressors remain triumphant
Gaza's people are forever stained
Grasping onto remains
Of what was
But no longer is prevalent
Their fight is one the world doesn't find relevant
As they die one by one
They fail to realize that the fight has just begun
We will rise
And aggrandize
Their stories
Filling up Gaza's ground with their names
Tending to the painful flame
Of the frustration
Angered by the deterioration
Of our land and our people
How could the world be so evil?
Displaying such malice
The people of Gaza deserve better than this
They deserve to live
Enjoy what life has to give
Not merely survive
But thrive
Strive
Yet they lack access to basic healthcare and operations

Clasping onto one another as they undergo painful amputations
Searching for any form of medication
To ease their ailments in such devastation
They scream at the loss of relatives
Their strain and exertion is evident
They are baffled as the world remains blind to their innocence
Their scars have stories that will take centuries to tell
To relay and portray to the world as we yell
Free Palestine
A statement implying that genocide is not fine
That the world will not remain compliant to murder and brutality
We will not pay mind to such insanity
Oh people of Gaza you no longer need to cry
You're suffering is known and you are going to be fine

I put my bag on my lap, laid my head down on it, and tried to get some sleep, longing for the trip to be over. Even the sound of my own breathing felt too loud—loud to the point of irritation, loud to the point where I could be heard.

Then, we stopped.

The air was stiff and smoky, and just being in Palestine, the fear was palpable. I was startled—we had already passed the checkpoints. Cautiously, I peered outside the window, and my heart stopped.

Two IDF soldiers.

Their eyes shone with malice, evident even in the way they walked—calculated, menacing. Both were armed and in uniform, standing outside with stern expressions, interrogating a flustered Jamal. They looked young, at most in their mid-twenties. One was tall and lanky, the other shorter and stockier with a solid build.

They ordered all the volunteers out of the truck, making them drop their belongings and put their hands on their heads. One by one, they meticulously searched through each bag. I curled into the side of the truck and made dua.

Jamal reached into his pocket to pull out some documents. The taller soldier immediately raised his gun, aiming it at him. His eyes narrowed, his mouth pressed into a tight line.

My heart stopped. My fingers grew clammy.

It was like those nightmares I used to have about Maryam and my parents. Only now, it was real. It was happening right in front of me. I was in Gaza—the land of my oppressed brothers and sisters, the center of my heart. And once again, the oppressors were abusing their power. But this time, I was there to witness it firsthand.

No amount of Instagram posts could have prepared me for that moment.

I wanted to scream. To say something. To do something.

But I clamped my hand over my mouth, realizing what that could mean for me.

"Please let us go," called out a volunteer named Yassin. "We are citizens of the United States and are authorized to be here by our government."

The soldier lowered his gun slightly. "What's in it for us if we let you go?"

Money. It was always about the money.

One by one, the volunteers emptied their pockets, pooling together a thick wad of cash in various currencies.

"This is all we have," Jamal pleaded. "Please, let us pass."

The soldiers took the cash, visibly satisfied.

"Wait," the shorter soldier said. "As soon as we see what's inside that truck, you can go."

My heart pounded. My forehead grew damp with sweat, and tears pricked my eyes. This was it. The end.

I would join my family in our sealed fate—the fate of every living human being.

I began repeating the shahadah, ensuring I would die a Muslim. The soldier moved toward the back of the truck, his flashlight scanning the space. I still had the boxes in front of me. Slowly, I turned my head and noticed a small gap leading to the front of the truck.

Without thinking, I wiggled through, holding my breath, and hid under the seats, whispering the shahadah over and over.

I realized how foolish I had been. I hadn't thought this through—I had acted on pure instinct.

How worried everyone must have been.

How could I have put all of us in danger?

The soldiers finished their search, slammed the truck shut, and walked away. I turned my face away, not daring to look in their direction. The volunteers didn't enter the truck until they were sure the soldiers were out of sight.

EPILOGUE

The rest of the journey is one I cannot disclose. It was a journey of reflection, of tears, of an encounter with the divine. Its continuation was nothing short of a miracle from Allah.

Did I die? He knows best.

All I know is that my life became a path of self-growth and introspection, shaping the evolution of my organization, my relationships, and the man I was yet to become. What I had done was an act of defiance—one that carried heavy consequences, yet brought me an inner peace I had never known.

I had started helpless, alone, vulnerable—staring into the sun, so much so that it could have dimmed me. But I ended in prostration, within the mosque of my dreams.

Maryam's dreams.

Since the day her life was taken, I had lived for both of us. Everything I did was for her, more than for myself.

I ended in sajdah, my eyes brimming with tears, whispering to my Lord. My family wept in gratitude, and I offered Salaam—peace—to the angels surrounding the space.

From fear to reassurance. From loneliness to togetherness. From hostility to camaraderie. This story was never mine alone.

The fulfillment of my lifelong dream was made possible by those by my side and those within my heart.

InshaAllah, may it serve as a means of further inspiration.